Gina was more than a little unnerved when the confident and autocratic Tod Fallon began to interfere with her television series. What was he doing there? And why was he apparently so interested in her?

FANTASY WOMAN

BY

ANNABEL MURRAY

MILLS & BOON LIMITED
15–16 BROOK'S MEWS
LONDON W1A 1DR

*First published in Great Britain 1986
by Mills & Boon Limited*

© Annabel Murray 1986

*Australian copyright 1986
Philippine copyright 1986
This edition 1986*

ISBN 0 263 75494 4

*Set in Monophoto Times 10 on 11 pt.
01–1086 – 55637*

*Typset in Great Britain by
Richard Clay (The Chaucer Press) Ltd,
Bungay, Suffolk
Printed and bound in Great Britain
by Collins, Glasgow*

CHAPTER ONE

'COME on! *Come on!* Damn you!'

It was an old saw that a watched kettle never boiled and it certainly seemed that the more constantly you looked at a clock, the slower its hands moved. Irritatingly, the clock in Tod Fallon's hotel suite was no exception.

He could have gone for a walk to pass away the time, but London was in one of its wet, cold, grey moods. So instead, for the last hour, he had been pacing up and down from bedroom to sitting-room, with a monotonous, regular tread that might have inflicted serious damage on a less expensive carpet. His rawly masculine features wore an expression of intense irritation at the tedious waiting; irritation also with himself, at his nervous, anticipatory mood, the necessity for expending his valuable time. Marcha would be furious if she knew what he was up to, but though, for the past six months, it had been his habit to indulge Marcha in every way, this time she must bend to *his* will.

He was unaccustomed to waiting; efficient aides, secretaries and household staff saw to that. But not even a man of his wealth, power and influence could hasten time, even though, to him, time was money and time was something that was running short, thanks to Marcha's procrastination.

During his pacing he had thrown off the jacket of his impeccably tailored grey suit, wrenched loose the knot of his tie and discarded it, too, the violence of the act also serving to undo the top buttons of his blue silk shirt, revealing that the smooth bronze of his facial skin extended down the hard, firmly corded throat to his

5

chest. His thick, dark, vibrant hair, liberally sprinkled with grey, had been disarrayed by the impatient, forceful thrusting of strong hands.

Tall and broad, physically dominating his surroundings, the energy and ill-suppressed eagerness exuding from him made even the generous proportions of his suite seem small and confining.

He picked up, for perhaps the twentieth time, the printed programme provided by the management; for all the suites in this luxury building boasted a television set. Though he could have recited its contents by heart, he re-read the blurb outlining the show he intended to watch. 'An extravaganza, produced in association with TLM Enterprises.' He studied intently the adjacent photograph of the presenter, a poor reproduction which did little to answer the numerous questions that exercised his mind. It was hard to believe she would be suitable, yet he had his secretary's firm assurance. Strange, though, that Marcha should be so against the idea.

An exasperated glance showed him that the hands of the clock had still barely moved and he threw aside the magazine, reaching for the television's remote control switch. Even the advertisements would be preferable to riding out this uncharacteristic tension.

Tod Fallon was accustomed to getting what he wanted. It was disconcerting to realise that this time he could not be one hundred per cent certain of attaining his objective. As the last of the adverts faded away and the music, the opening credits, of the next programme began, Tod found himself leaning forward, poised on the edge of his seat, and with an exclamation of annoyance he forced himself to relax. Damn it! He shouldn't have any doubts. If his own findings confirmed what his secretary had told him, his eventual object would be achieved. After all, he was in a position to pull several influential strings.

Only a fool would turn down the proposal he intended to make.

An anonymous voice, overlaid with dramatic emphasis made the announcement,

'Every week, millions of viewers tune in to this station to see her, the lady to whom no request is an impossibility. Ladies and gentlemen, viewers everywhere, your presenter, Fantasy Woman!'

To studio applause, she appeared, walking down, around the turn of a spiralling staircase, and this time Tod was unaware of his own forward inclination as his intelligent dark eyes scanned and assessed the star of the show. What age would she be? About twenty-five? Was that too old for what he had in mind? Television could be deceptive, but he guessed she was the right height, around five-seven, five-eight, long-legged, and frankly curvaceous, with firm, splendid breasts emphasised by the cut and drape of the sparkling evening gown she wore. Thick, almost straight hair, the colour of a red setter's coat, framed all that he could see of her face. If only the damned woman didn't have to wear that half mask. But his secretary had warned him about that ridiculous gimmick.

So far, she was just what he'd been led to expect. Her figure would have done justice to a Miss World candidate. Despite the mask, he could discern that her face was square, with a chin as uncompromisingly determined as his own—a little too strong perhaps for someone whom he intended to manipulate—and that below the lower edge of the black square her mouth was wide and generously proportioned.

The programme planners had certainly spared no expense, either on the lavish set or on her glamorous outfit; and the same applied to the stunts, the fulfilment of wishes. A young girl wanted to meet a favourite pop star. Others were more bizarre, such as the ninety-year-old woman who had always wanted to ride a camel.

There were the wildly extravagant, the comic; some were even looking for the excitement of danger. As he watched, Tod's eyebrows, a thick dark line, came down heavily above brooding eyes and he nodded decisively. This woman he had to meet, and if she was any good ...

Gina Darcy lowered her long, graceful length into the only comfortable chair in her dressing-room and peeled off the black mask which, with her make-up and the perspiration caused by strong studio lights, had adhered unpleasantly to her face. She was always glad to be rid of the wretched thing, wished she need not wear it, but her sponsors were adamant. It was part of her image, of the anonymity behind which she hid, the apparently all-powerful Fantasy Woman.

That was a joke! If only people knew it. Not that she didn't enjoy her role, but sometimes she wished it had greater depth of involvement; wished that the fame, the nationwide acclaim, could be for Gina Darcy and not for her *alter ego*; two minor adjustments to her role which the sponsors had always refused to consider.

There was one advantage: no one from her old life was likely to recognise her. The most likely people to guess her identity from her voice and general appearance, her parents, were living abroad. Even Keith was unlikely to see, in her glamorous new identity, the old Gina. In one sense that was a source of dissatisfaction. She would *like* Keith to see her, to realise that she had made a success of her life, despite and without him. But her real name was never printed in the programme and thus far, following instructions, she had managed to evade and baffle the press. Still, she thought, stretching her body in a movement as languorous and graceful as a cat's, apart from the frustrated ambition to be famous in her own right, as Marcha had become, she had a lot to be thankful for:

her career in television and, discreetly in the background, a thriving business of her own, to which she could return if this life ever palled.

Not that she thought it would. She was busy, fulfilled, mistress of her own destiny, with no one other than her producer to interfere or to criticise her, no man to make demands of her; and if that was selfish, well, Gina considered she had earned her right to be so. She'd been self-sacrificing once and all that had brought was unhappiness and disillusionment.

A knock on her dressing-room door, the insertion of a glaringly ginger head and a pleasant, freckled face, heralded the arrival of Jimmy Riley, originator and executive producer of *Fantasy Woman*. Only he and the programme's sponsors were aware of Gina's true identity; there was Marcha, of course, but she'd been sworn to secrecy.

'Superb performance as ever, darling!' His voice was affectionate, his lean face full of enthusiasm. Precariously, he perched his long, wiry frame on a stool, too alight with nervous energy and excitement to take up any more permanent position.

'Yes, thank goodness!' The words, spoken in a warm, husky voice, were heartfelt. 'I'd much prefer it if the programme was all prerecorded items. When we go out live, you can never be sure something won't go wrong.'

'Hmm!' Jimmy did not sound convinced. 'On the other hand, our viewers like the live shows, the element of chance. Keeps them on the edge of their seats. Which reminds me . . . .' He pulled a sheet of paper from his jacket pocket. 'Thought you might like to see next week's schedule.'

As Gina perused the list, Jimmy watched her intently, studying her reactions. Her square, vivid face was so tellingly expressive, he thought, as always feeling himself deeply stirred by her attraction. Beautiful woman! Pity they had to disguise half the potential of those lovely features.

Gina had a large following. Fan mail arrived for her daily by the sackful, and the programme was inundated with requests from people wanting to be on her show. Not surprisingly, there was a high ratio of requests from curious men, but *they* were flogging a dead horse. Stage door Johnnies weren't encouraged, and, under the terms of Gina's contract, personal involvement with any of her guests was strictly forbidden. Not that there was any danger of Gina flouting the rule. As far as Jimmy could see, Gina didn't go in for personal relationships of any kind. He had never heard her mention her family or any women friends, and her reactions to men were all too clear.

He had particular reason to know that much. Strongly attracted to Gina, he had once tried to push their relationship beyond the bounds of producer and presenter, but only once. Gina had been perfectly polite but, nevertheless, she had made it quite clear that she was not interested. It was nothing personal, she'd explained, her tone coolly remote, simply that she had no intention of becoming involved with any man. She had her future mapped out. First and last, she intended to remain a career woman.

So chilly had been the barriers she erected that Jimmy had not even dared to ask why, for he guessed there must be some other reason besides ambition. He didn't believe for one moment that she was frigid. It was his theory that, at some time in the past, Gina had been badly hurt by a man and that she didn't intend to risk a similar occurrence.

But what a waste! She was a woman formed for love, and he wasn't just thinking of the physical side. She was a thoroughly nice person, caring and compassionate. She really enjoyed making people happy, especially kids. She would have made a wonderful mother.

Her smooth brow had furrowed into creases and he could guess why. He'd known she wasn't going to like one of the items on that list, but there was nothing he could do. The sponsors' word was law.

'This motor-cycle scramble, the fifteen-year-old girl who wants to compete against the boys . . .'

'I know what you're going to say, Gina, but it's no use. It's in. The girl's been contacted, so have the organisers of the rally. All *you* have to do is to *be* there, introduce the item, congratulate her or console her afterwards as the case may be and hand over the "Fantasy" memento.'

'It could be dangerous for the kid,' Gina began.

Jimmy sighed. With variations of theme, they had this same argument almost weekly.

'Nowhere near as risky as some of the stunts we used to pull. We do weed out the really dangerous ones nowadays. At the worst, the kid'll get a few bumps and bruises and a sore behind. The sponsors . . .'

'To hell with the sponsors!' she interrupted impatiently. 'They think they're little tin gods, but they're just damned irresponsible. It won't be one of them that gets the blame, or the pain, if there's an accident. If that kid gets injured, perhaps for life, it will be the programme that gets the bad publicity and I'll carry the can, too. I've never forgotten . . .' She shuddered, not finishing her sentence.

'Yes, well,' Jimmy put in hastily, 'the incident you're thinking of had its effect even on the sponsors. They won't permit anything like that again and'—as she looked to be on the point of arguing further—'you know it's no good your standing out against them. They reserve the power to hire and fire. What's the point in risking losing your job? You still enjoy it, don't you?' And *he* didn't want to lose her, he thought painfully.

'You know I still enjoy it and I don't want to lose it;

and I know I'm not irreplaceable. That damned mask sees to that. I'm not the first to wear it and I know, if I were to quit or get fired, I wouldn't be the last. The name Fantasy Woman will fit anyone with a reasonable figure and red hair. But Jimmy, if only they'd let me try out some of the stunts, test them before these kids risk their necks. And I'm getting tired of being an anonymous figure. One of these days, I want to be a show-business personality in my own right, as me, Gina Darcy. I want to show the public that I'm more than just a body, a figure-head.'

Jimmy shrugged. He wasn't complaining about the figure she presented, but, if she only knew it, with her looks and bubbling personality she had the potential to go a long way. She had more than looks, a kind of sparkle; but to himself he could admit that, in part, he was responsible for holding her back, that her anonymity suited him. He had a selfish desire to keep Gina to himself. He hadn't given up hope that some day he'd persuade her to . . . Aloud, he said, not unaware of hypocrisy,

'As a friend, as well as your producer, I'd advise against any change at present, not while you're still so popular in this role, while the show's still going down well. Some day, maybe, hmm?'

'You mean when I start getting old and wrinkled? When they decide to replace me with someone younger? Then you'll have me playing old-lady character parts? No thanks! Rather than wait for that to happen, I'll go back and carry on running my business.'

'I meant,' he interrupted hastily, 'when you're established enough for the public to want to see you in other roles.'

'How are they supposed to express their wishes,' she demanded sarcastically, 'when they don't even know what I look like? I could be as ugly as sin.'

'There's no guarantee that you'd be a success in other fields.'

'And there's always the fact that this show is your baby,' Gina retorted. Then, penitently, 'Sorry, Jimmy, that was uncalled for. I know your advice is well-meant, but sometimes I get so frustrated. I know I have it in me to do better things.'

'And you know, too,' he added drily, 'that if I had my way, you'd never work at all. I can well afford to support a wife and . . .'

'Jimmy, please!' she said hurriedly. Not that well-worn track again. She'd heard those words so often before, interminably. 'Don't start. Don't ruin our friendship. Nowadays you're the only man I've any respect for.'

His pleasure mingling with guilt, he shrugged himself off the stool.

'I suppose that's something,' he conceded wryly. Then, consulting his watch, 'Well, the fans should have given up by now. Time to go home.'

Gina always waited for an hour after the studio audience had left. Only once had she tried to leave immediately and she had run the gamut of a curious, sensation-seeking crowd. One man had even tried to snatch off her mask. These days she left the TV centre dressed shabbily, a scarf tightly obscuring the giveaway cascade of red hair, Jimmy driving her back to her flat in a deliberately unostentatious car. Now, the only other time she wore the mask was on location, when she was surrounded by the protective posse of cameramen and the production team.

'Any chance of a coffee?' Jimmy enquired, as they pulled up outside the block of flats near Regents Park which housed her bachelor apartment.

Amused, for it was a regular request which he already knew would not be granted, she shook her head.

'Fantasy Woman,' he quoted grumblingly, 'never

says no! Never says impossible. Except to poor old Jimmy Riley.'

Laughter faded from her lovely face as she slid from the passenger seat.

'Now you know that's not true, Jimmy, not in my private life. No one has seen the inside of my little flat except my cleaning lady, and to her, I'm just "Miss Darcy" who's "something in the City"!'

'You can't blame a chap for trying!' Jimmy said glumly and her amusement returned.

'And *you* can't blame a girl for being consistent! 'Night, Jimmy!'

'Little flat' was a purposely inadequate description of her four-room apartment. Like her past and her private life, she chose to keep her surroundings strictly to herself, a place where she could be herself, with no one else making their mark upon it, leaving memories to destroy the peaceful atmosphere she had created and which closed about her in a reassuring cocoon every time she came home.

With a sigh of relief she closed the apartment door behind her, shutting out the world, shutting out fantasy. What, she wondered, would her fans think if they ever discovered how different was the woman from the public image? She suspected that most of the people she interviewed found her daunting, thought of her as the kind of woman who would always have everything under control. Because, in her name, their fantasies were fulfilled, they probably believed her infallible where her own life was concerned. They were wrong; at least, they were wrong about the past.

But that mistake was behind her, never to be repeated. For the future all her energies and emotions would be wrapped up in her career. Only once had she let her heart rule her head, dropping ambition for what she had mistakenly expected to be personal happiness.

There would be no more Keiths to dispute her right to her individuality and independence and then, finally, worst blow of all, to destroy her confidence in herself as a woman.

She wandered into the modern, functional kitchen, walls, units and ceiling in stainless steel, and collected the items she needed to make herself a snack. Did her former husband ever think of her these days? Did he ever speak of her to Frances, making comparisons that would not be in Gina's favour? She'd met Frances just once; an insignificant little woman, the type who would fulfil Keith's notion of a 'proper wife': placid, domesticated and, perhaps even more important in view of his nature, unlikely to attract admiring notice from other men.

Ironically, now that she was not forced into a domestic role, Gina enjoyed her free time, experimenting with recipes in her streamlined kitchen; doing her own decorating; looking after her enormous collection of plants, which, growing in a variety of exotic pots, stood on a raised semi-circular dais under the living-room window.

She was entitled to enjoy her leisure! She worked hard, five days a week, researching, rehearsing and, quite often, filming on location, as she would have to at the motor-cycle rally.

She gave an irritated exclamation. She tried not to bring working problems home with her, but this one worried her, nearly as much as that other incident which had had near-fatal results.

She took her snack supper into the luxurious sitting-room, feeling her usual sense of satisfaction at its sybaritic comfort. Decorated in harmonising shades of green, it had a sunken central square of cushions; the shelving around the wall held valuable antiques. She sat down among the cushions, in her favourite place, the position from which she could best admire her small, but precious, collection of Impressionist paintings. When she'd been seventeen, she reflected wryly, weekend evenings had been for dating. Staying in had been a tragedy, not having a date a social stigma. But all those agonies were gone. Supper for one in front of the television was a pleasure nowadays, not a pain. Who needed men?

'Gina, you are incredible!' Jimmy said, one morning a few days later, as she joined him in the rain-sodden field, the mud already churned ankle deep by the spinning wheels of motor cycles.

'Ssh!' Anxiously, automatically, she looked about her, seeking possible eavesdroppers. It was customary for her to be addressed only as Fantasy Woman. Satisfied that no one was within earshot, she asked, 'What do you mean?'

'I mean that only you could contrive to look both sexy and mysterious in the middle of a muddy field, wearing blue waterproofs, red wellingtons and *that hat*!'

She laughed aloud.

'What you forget, Jimmy, is that, basically, I *am* the outdoor type!'

Her delighted laughter, throaty, husky, had carried clearly on the damp morning air, and Tod Fallon, already alerted to her arrival by the cavalcade of cars and vans, the swivelling of cameras, the anticipatory murmurs that had run through the watching crowd, edged his way imperceptibly closer. She seemed to be on good terms with the ginger-headed fellow at her elbow. Boyfriend? Unlikely from what he'd heard about her. Probably part of the production team. Whoever he was, Tod decided, he wasn't man enough to handle *that* redheaded package of dynamite.

There was even less of her visible today, he thought, with a return of his irritation. Muffled up in a voluminous blue cagoule, the top half of her face

obscured by the mask and the black, waterproof
sombrero, all that showed was the laughing mouth: a
wide, generous sweep of full lips, exposing white, even
teeth.

In view of the weather, he had expected feminine
petulance, moodiness, from the star of the show, but
she looked and sounded remarkably cheerful. Still, she
could afford to be cheerful. He had been pulling those
confidential strings and he now had some idea of just
how much she earned from this series and from the by-
products of her personality cult; her earnings reached a
figure that some people would find hard to match. But
not Tod Fallon. Finance presented no problem to him.
Besides, everyone had their price, and he had the best of
incentives to bid high . . . Marcha!

In spite of the steady drizzle, which had seemed to
reduce everything and everyone to the same uniform
grey, Gina had noticed Tod Fallon. He would be a
difficult man to overlook. Even in casual, weatherproof
clothes, his height made him stand out in this motley
crowd; he was totally unlike the usual run of sensation
seekers. He looked too cultured, too sophisticated
somehow, to be interested in her or her show, or even in
today's events. Unless, of course, he was the bored but
indulgent parent of one of the young participants. Most
of these motor-cycle-mad kids had families who could
afford to buy them the best, the latest model of bike.
There must be at least a dozen of the machines here
today, a kaleidoscope of varying metallic colours,
circling and recircling the assembly point, practising
'wheelies', churning up the mud, the drone of high
revving engines monotonous to the ear, wearing on the
nerves.

Oh, let's get on with it, she thought suddenly, get it
safely over. She felt the usual butterflies churn in the pit
of her stomach. She hated this waiting. Would she

never forget the stunt that had gone so tragically
wrong? No! Impossible! Not even if she were to neglect
her self-imposed, regular reminder of it.

Inevitably there was a lot of waiting around on
location shots, waiting for cameramen to decide on
angles; and today they would wait while one or two of
the regular kids were filmed going over the course, just
to show how tricky it really was, wheels spinning
helplessly on muddy inclines, bunny hopping over logs,
easing their way beneath tricky limbos. Then it would
be the 'victim's' turn. Despite the waterproof, some of
the damp chill must have got through to her, for she
shivered a little. Physically fearless herself, she would
far rather be waiting to undergo the ordeal than to see
if someone else, particularly a youngster, came safely
through it.

Her curious gaze returned several times to Tod
Fallon's strong, compelling face, as she speculated on
who and what he was, why he was here. For some
reason he interested her; in a purely academic way, of
course. Because she shunned male company for herself,
it didn't mean she couldn't appreciate a man's
appearance, feel curiosity about his character and
occupation.

This one was a little too spectacular-looking for her
taste, with his splendid physique and those dark good
looks, enhanced rather than marred by the generous
scattering of grey hair. Such men, she'd always found,
were arrogantly aware of their own masculine attrac-
tions. He looked a tough character, too, with those
rugged features and that assertive chin. Not the sort
you'd care to tangle with. The heavy black bar of
eyebrows that just met across the straight, forthright
nose, hinted at an intolerant nature, a hasty temper that
it would be unwise to arouse.

Suddenly she realised that the prolonged analysis had
not been one-way. *He* was watching *her*, his study more

covert than her own, as though to avoid detection. But now she had discovered his ploy, he met her eyes openly, almost challengingly. No doubt he was accustomed to women giving him more than a second glance, was probably complacent and conceited about the fact. She too was accustomed to appreciation, male appreciation, which these days she shrugged aside. But why did she have the feeling that this man was not just admiring, that there was more to his assessment than that?

As his piercing eyes continued to hold hers, she realised that he was moving slowly but surely towards her, that, despite a supreme effort of will, she could not break the tenuous link between them. She felt more than just a slight unease now. He must have taken her idle curiosity for interest, invitation even?

'Jimmy,' she murmured, 'that man; he's getting too close.' But for once Jimmy was out of earshot. 'That's far enough,' she told the man, politely but coldly, so that there should be no mistaking the fact that she meant what she said.

'Surely there can be no objection to my paying homage to . . . a celebrity?' The pause before the final words was mocking. Why on earth should a total stranger speak to her in this way?

'No objection,' she conceded coolly, 'but if you have anything to say, you can say it from where you are.'

'Right!' To her relief, he seemed to accept her dictum. 'First off, what's the purpose of the mask?' Tod asked bluntly. He knew the purpose very well, but he wanted to gauge her reaction to provocation. 'Are you disfigured?'

'No I'm not!' Energetically, Gina refuted the suggestion. But just suppose she had been? What a totally unfeeling brute of a man he must be!

'Then why?' he persisted.

'I thought everyone knew that by now,' she retorted

scornfully. 'It's to preserve Fantasy Woman's anonymity.'

'I've been out of the country for a while,' Tod said. 'Last week was only the first time I've watched your programme. It's not,' he added drily, 'my normal taste in viewing.'

I bet, Gina thought. He was probably an intellectual snob. The news and heavy documentaries would be about his only concession to the popular medium. But all levels had to be catered for and her programme provided a service to those who liked their entertainment light.

'I don't see the need for such a ridiculous charade,' Tod continued. 'Other presenters don't seem to find it necessary and there *are* very similar programmes.'

'Exactly!' she said triumphantly. 'So we need something different, a gimmick.' What was she doing, she wondered in amazement, defending the particular aspect of the show that she herself most disliked? It must be that this man made her hackles rise. She felt she would have taken issue with him on any subject.

'A feeble reason,' the big man retorted. 'Now, if you were afraid of being recognised outside the studio, that I *could* understand.'

'Why should I be afraid?' Gina challenged him.

'Oh, I don't know. Let's say something went wrong on your show? Wouldn't people blame you for any accidents? Threaten you even? The public can be very fickle where their idols are concerned. Just suppose this kid today breaks a leg or something?'

'Are you a reporter?' Gina asked suspiciously. 'Because if so, I don't give interviews.' It was a little late to make a stand on that principle, she thought, furious with herself. He'd already elicited enough information from her to write an article, embroidering it, misquoting her.

'I'm not a reporter and you haven't answered my question.'

'I don't have to answer your question, but just to put the record straight I'll tell you what you want to know and then perhaps you'll kindly stop pestering me. Things very rarely do go wrong. Stunts are always supervised by experts.'

'But there have been incidents?' Tod persisted, 'Injuries?'

'One or two, nothing serious, not since I . . .'

'OK, Fantasy Woman!' One of the cameramen sang out. 'We're ready to take the opening shots.'

Relieved, Gina turned away from her inquisitor. Briefly, she filled Jimmy in on the incident.

'Where were you when I needed you?' she reproached. 'I wonder who he is and why he was asking all those questions? He sounded as if he disapproved of the show, of me.'

'He'll be press of some kind, whatever he says. Forget him! It's time for the introduction. We'll have you sitting on one of these bikes, I think.'

'Why not have her carry out the stunt herself? Just to show how safe and easy it is?'

Gina swung around with a gasp of stupefaction, every sense suddenly wary and alert. The tall man had followed them, was at her elbow, only inches separating them. She felt herself tauten and quiver, almost as if he had touched her, unwelcomely conscious of the strong aura of masculinity that had been apparent even at a distance. She felt overpowered. She was tall, but he was taller. To her suddenly vibrating nerves, it seemed he exuded a kind of subtle menace.

'Will you please keep your distance, sir!' Jimmy was annoyed.

'Has your Fantasy Woman ever tried out any of the things she expects her guests to do?' Tod persisted, quite undeterred apparently by their joint hostile reaction.

'I don't expect people to do anything,' Gina snapped,

before Jimmy could answer. 'They ask me to arrange something. After that it's up to them.'

'So you don't care if they injure themselves?'

'Of course I'd care if someone was hurt.' Gina felt uncharacteristically close to tears, and she hadn't wept since . . . Oh, why did he have to set her nerves jangling just at this moment, when she was already tense?

'But you're too chicken to try the stunts yourself?'

'No! No! No! Will you stop pestering me? I'm not scared of anything! But the terms of my contract don't permit me to . . . Oh, go away! I've got a show to do.'

Determined that this arrogant, pushy man should not witness the distress he was causing her, she swung away, then felt her feet in their bright wellingtons slip from under her so that she sprawled her length in the cycle-churned mud. Before Jimmy could move to help her, the tall man had done so, his hands closing about her upper arms, hauling her unceremoniously to her feet. Gina felt like screaming with frustration. Her bright blue cagoule was soiled and, although she wasn't hurt physically, her pride was severely damaged. She'd made a fool of herself in front of all these people. It would be in every paper tomorrow, unless someone more important had an equally ridiculous accident. It was all this man's fault, she fumed. If he hadn't been so annoyingly persistent, made her angry, she wouldn't have moved so carelessly.

The heat of fury banished the tears that had threatened and she looked up, intent upon scorching him both verbally and with her eyes. Lips parted, the stream of invective she had planned was silenced by the mirth in his hitherto serious face. He was silently laughing at her! How dared he! Then, to add insult to injury, he gave vent to his amusement in a great shout, plainly audible to every bystander.

'Fantasy Woman!' he spluttered, scarcely able to articulate. 'Whatever happened to that air of dignified mystery? Right at this moment, you look more like a disreputable Paddington Bear!'

Gina gasped with outrage, but then the aptness, the ludicrous truth of his statement struck her and against her will her own sense of the ridiculous surfaced. She felt her mouth begin to quirk with the beginnings of a smile, a smile swiftly banished by his next words.

'That's better. At least it proves you're human, that you can laugh at your own misfortunes as well as those of others. Now, if I could only see what you look like, without that mask . . .'

But she backed away hastily, carefully this time, and to her relief he did not pursue her any further. But Gina was aware of his dark eyes watching the filming from the distance Jimmy insisted on for all members of the public, and annoyingly she found his words rankling with her.

At school and in her teens, she'd been a splendid athlete, horsewoman and swimmer; and she'd always kept herself fit. Recently, she had even been attending judo classes. She knew she was capable of feats of physical endurance, so why couldn't that dimension be added to the show?

As for the stranger's accusation that she laughed at the failures of others, she was frankly puzzled. It was something she wouldn't dream of doing, however comical such an incident might be. Like most people, she possessed the banana-skin sense of humour, but to give vent to it at the expense of her guests would be most unprofessional. It puzzled her, too, why this man seemed so set on annoying her.

Automatically, she went through the typical intro-ductory script. The young motor cyclists performed. The girl who had made the request to compete against the boys did so and acquitted herself reasonably well. The shots were in the can and the episode would be one of many shown on the next programme. Nothing further untoward occurred. The large man would have to eat his words, admit that safety was a major factor of their undertakings.

But there was no sign of him and, where she should havé felt relieved, Gina felt unreasonably disappointed. It would have been pleasant to have given him a triumphant 'I told you so' look. It would at least have redressed some of the indignity of her own mishap.

CHAPTER TWO

THAT evening, she found her mind returning over and over again to the stranger's suggestion, a suggestion that, had he but known it, matched strongly with her own inclinations.

Without much hope, once again, she had broached the subject with Jimmy, and as usual he had been frankly horrified.

'Sorry, it's not on. The sponsors wouldn't allow it. If you started performing stunts, we'd have a totally different programme concept. And if it's that fellow that accosted you this morning, forget him. There's no reason for you to worry what he thinks. Is there?' he added suspiciously.

Gina sighed with exasperation. She was letting work intrude on her free time yet again, and this time it was the fault of that annoying man. Hoping to divert her thoughts, she switched on the television. At this time of night, there was usually something purely escapist, a laughable rather than spine-chilling horror film, or some corny soap opera.

It was the latter, set in a totally unbelievable hospital. None of the incidents shown could possibly happen in real life, would never have been permitted to happen in the hospital where she had once worked.

For, originally, Gina had intended to be a nurse. She'd just completed her first year, when she met Keith Taylor. A journalist, he'd come to the hospital to cover a heart transplant operation and Gina had been the only person passing through reception. He'd delayed his appointment with the hospital secretary just long enough to fix his image upon the impressionable

25

nineteen-year-old she'd been then, and had managed to intercept her once more on his way out, to ask her for a date.

It had been a whirlwind romance and, against all advice, she had married Keith within six weeks of their first encounter. Too late she'd realised that married life was not all that she had anticipated. Things had started to go wrong, even on their honeymoon.

Following almost immediately upon Gina's disillusionment with married life, there had been drastic cuts in the health service and she and many of her fellow students had found themselves unemployed.

Keith had been delighted; now she would be totally dependent on him. During their brief courtship, he'd managed to disguise certain traits which, since marriage, had come unpleasantly to the fore. He was possessive and almost dangerously jealous. Not only had he been jealous; he hadn't been satisfied with her as she was, the girl he professed to love, but had tried to mould her into his conception of a wife. Perhaps all men had this desire for dominance, the need to change the status quo? That man at the rally! Hadn't he been suggesting change and hadn't she disliked his attitude towards herself? She resented male scorn, the assumption of male superiority.

The video of the girl motor cyclist was popular with the following week's studio audience. It was usual to have one live item and the rest of the events were prerecorded. The show was going successfully and yet, somehow, Gina felt dissatisfied.

She knew she was looking more than usually stunning tonight. Apart from the fact that she had no time for false modesty, other eyes besides her own had told her so—those of the cameramen; the indrawn breath of the audience had been complimentary; and earlier, in her dressing-room, Jimmy had been lavish with his praise.

Her new outfit, a sensational, sparkling gold two-piece, fitted her like a second skin that echoed every movement of her voluptuous figure. Dolman sleeved, it had a plunging V-back top. Dramatic, high-heeled black shoes and daring black-seamed stockings completed the outfit. Yes, she looked good.

Yet all the time she laughed and joked with her guests, introduced their particular fantasies, another part of her mind held itself aloof, trying to analyse her dissatisfaction. There had been no mishaps so far and there were not likely to be; the mixture was as before. 'As before.' That was it! The show was becoming boringly predictable! It was time to inject a new dimension, but she was the only one who seemed to feel this way. Everyone else seemed happy, the guests, the audience, the production team. Out of camera shot, she could just see Jimmy's freckled face, set in complacent lines. Was she the only one to notice something lacking?

Then the penny dropped. It was all the fault of that damned man at the motor-cycle rally. That crack of his about her being too cowardly to try the stunts herself, the implication, with which secretly she had agreed, that she could make much more of her role. But to be honest, it wasn't entirely his fault she felt this way. She'd already begun to think along similar lines with her urge to shed her anonymity.

'And now,' the voice of the unseen announcer broke in upon her thoughts, 'a slight variation from our usual routine, a request that even Fantasy Woman herself knows nothing about.'

Gina jerked to attention; illogically her first reaction was one of indignation. How dared they spring something on her for which she was unprepared? And who had arranged for the gratification of the request, whatever it was? It was unprecedented; she'd never had to cope with the unexpected. Could she do it when she had no idea what was wanted of her?

Then the stubborn chin came into prominence. Of course she could. Besides, Jimmy would have arranged things. He wouldn't really have left everything to chance. Feeling about her as he did, he wouldn't permit anyone to make her look foolish.

So she donned a smile of sweet unconcern for the cameras; but, outwardly calm, inwardly she was in a turmoil of curiosity.

The introduction continued.

'People ask many things of Fantasy Woman: the simple, the outrageous, the ordinary, the bizarre, cheap or expensive. But no guest has ever asked for anything so easy to bestow and yet, he obviously thinks, and you the audience will surely agree, beyond price.'

The build up was making Gina uneasy and when the 'guest' came into sight, her unease grew. It was *that man*. A superstitious shudder cooled her spine. It was almost as if she'd conjured him up.

He was within inches of her now, broad, brown, powerfully built, exuding masculine virility, his slacks and shirt deceptively casual. He hadn't bought them in any chain store, or off the peg!

As she renewed her acquaintance with that square-cut jaw, looked once more into those glinting dark eyes, Gina felt again that almost primitive surge of fear. She wanted to turn and run. Instead she forced herself to remember who and where she was, parted her lips in a stiff parody of her usual welcoming smile and, with only an instant's hesitation, extended her slim hand.

'Good evening, Mr ...?' So far had they deviated from the norm, she didn't even know her guest's name.

He smiled and Gina, fascinated against her will, saw that only one corner of his mouth curved upwards, a crooked, tantalisingly attractive smile.

'You're not the only one who prefers anonymity.' His deep voice had a mocking note. 'Call me Mr X.'

He watched her work that one out, amused at her annoyance which was obvious from her physical reactions, a straightening of the spine, an upward surge of that chin, rather than from any facial expression, which was camouflaged by the mask. How would she respond? Had she the spirit to retaliate in public? If she incurred the censure of her sponsors it could make *his* job rather easier. But it didn't really matter. Things would go his way in the end. They always did.

If he wanted to play it this way, it was OK by Gina. She had no wish to know anything further about him. By force of will, she kept the pleasant expression pinned to her face.

'And what can we do for you, *Mr X*?' She laid sarcastic stress on his pseudonym, to let him know she ridiculed his pretension.

'What *you* can do for *me* . . .' he paused for effect, 'is to give me just one kiss.'

To a man, the audience drew an anticipatory breath, but an aghast Gina acted instinctively. She stepped backwards. The cameras followed her movement. So did he.

'A very simple request, surely?' he suggested, undertones in his dark, resonant voice that made her shudder. His whole aura had suddenly become one of brooding sensuality, and she knew she would give almost anything not to have to agree to his demand. Why had he made it? What did a kiss from her mean to him?

'An unusual request,' she parried. If it had been any other man, she would have been totally unconcerned; his request would have been granted by now, the kiss casually bestowed, the incident over, herself unaffected by it. But within Gina, something screamed a warning. She didn't want this man to kiss her. For she knew instinctively that she wouldn't be the one doing the kissing. This man was one hundred per cent male, very much the type to take the initiative.

Tod waited. He knew she wanted to refuse. Dared she? It didn't matter to him either way; it was merely a preliminary to getting under her guard, getting to know more about her, discovering whether she was as suitable as his secretary had suggested; and he paid his staff to be right, to give him reliable information. He frowned slightly. Marcha wouldn't approve of what he was doing. But what was one kiss bestowed in the interests of research, in Marcha's interests if only she would accept the fact? Suddenly he longed to have her back from her protracted holiday, this business concluded, to get on with the real purpose of his life.

'Well?' he challenged. 'What are you afraid of? Have you never kissed a man before?'

The audience tittered.

As he'd guessed, Gina wanted to refuse. But she couldn't. Fantasy Woman never denied a request. They were going out live, millions of viewers waiting expectantly to see her perform. If she turned down something so simple, her popularity, the show's popularity, would plummet, the viewing ratings would drop, the sponsors would be furious and the newspapers would have a field day, leaping upon the unprecedented incident with delight.

She gave one desperate look towards the side of the set, at Jimmy. He was also making frantic 'winding up' signals. They were running out of time. It was now or never.

Drawing a shaky breath, she moved in, placed her hands on the tall man's shoulders, looked up at him enquiringly.

For a second, Tod stared into the apprehensive eyes, shadowed by the mask. He could not discern their colour. He smiled and once more Gina felt the goose steps traverse her spine. Then the smile was blotted out, as his dark head swooped down towards her and hard, muscled arms clamped about her with a relentless pressure, so that her breasts were painfully entrapped against his ribcage. She was aware of many things in that moment, of the soft appreciative murmurs of the audience, the heat of the studio lights, the pleasant, tangy smell of male aftershave as his hand traced the silky skin that covered her spine. Then his mouth captured hers, hard, possessive, inescapable, the kiss burning in its intensity.

Shockwave after shockwave jerked her body in a totally unexpected, spasmodic response to the eroticism of his kiss, of his body moulded to hers. Being pressed so tightly against him was evocative of past sensations she'd believed banished, forgotten. But the ache in her loins was unmistakably familiar. Familiar, yet different. Keith had never made her feel like this . . . abandoned. She felt shame that such sensations could be aroused by a total stranger.

She was not the only one surprised by the effect of that kiss. Tod had gone into this embrace in a spirit of cynicism, it being his belief that a woman was more easily won over to a cause by an appeal, not to reason, on which most women were short, but to her sensuality. It wouldn't trouble him unduly if Gina Darcy responded favourably to the proposal he intended to put to her, just because she was attracted to him, rather than to the proposition. He'd been the victor in many such encounters and it was easy enough, after the battle was won, to depress any pretensions the woman might have. So it was with incredulity that he found himself strangely affected by the feel of Gina in his arms, the warmth and scent of her, the sudden, pliant softness of her body, as, against her will, she responded to him. Unexpectedly, he felt his body stir and, instinctively, he drew her closer, deepening the kiss.

Dimly, Gina heard the whistles and catcalls from the audience, realised that the kiss had gone on far too long, was becoming too intense. The theme music was playing. They were no longer on camera. Somehow she tore herself free of him and wondered that her legs should hold her, so limp and lifeless they felt.

'You swine!' she whispered. 'How *dare* you take advantage of me like that with the whole country watching?'

Tod was swifter to recover his composure. Thank God Marcha was abroad and not likely to be of that number. She certainly wouldn't have appreciated the little scene. And she'd been wrong about one thing; Gina Darcy certainly wasn't frigid.

'Really?' he drawled. 'You do rate your popularity high!'

Unable to utter another syllable, she swept past him, making for the sanctuary of her dressing-room. She passed Jimmy without even a look. He was to blame, too. He had known. He could have warned her. He was as bad as the rest of them. All he thought about was ratings, his wretched show. God, how she despised all men, especially this one! 'Mr X' was trouble! It didn't occur to her to wonder why her reaction to this particular man was so violent, why she had so arbitrarily assessed his character.

Later, at home, after a shower and a meal, she had calmed down a little, could look at the incident more rationally. She had taken out most of her anger on Jimmy during the drive home, but now that anger had evaporated, she felt curiously empty, drained.

'He went too far!' she'd raged. 'It was like being publicly raped.'

Jimmy had done his best to placate her. The item was by special request of the sponsors, he'd said, and he hadn't seen any real harm in it. After all, what was a kiss? Though even while he spoke the words, he knew he could almost hate the self-styled Mr X; would have given anything to be himself the recipient of Gina's kiss.

'OK. So he did make a meal of it,' he soothed, 'but, as a red-blooded male myself, I can't say I blame him, and maybe he didn't know the cameras had stopped rolling.'

'Oh, he knew,' Gina seethed. *'He knew!'*

What was a kiss, Jimmy had said. Before tonight, Gina would have answered, 'absolutely nothing', that a man's kiss was as unmoving as that of a maiden aunt. But she couldn't claim that now. Mr X was a past master of sensuality. She prayed the cameras had stopped filming before that moment when he'd used his tongue as a weapon to pierce her lips, probing, inciting her to unwilling response. She prayed the camera hadn't picked up the instinctive movements of her body, the heat which had flushed her face and throat, as she knew, for the first time in over a year, the wild compulsion of physical desire.

She couldn't fathom his motive, but she hoped to goodness he was satisfied, that she need never encounter him again; and yet, all evening, she found her thoughts returning to the incident, as a tongue returns to worry an aching tooth, her body reacting to the mental stimulus.

It was a week or two before Gina could relax, convince herself that Mr X was not going to make any further unheralded appearances; and then, annoyingly, she found herself wondering why he had abandoned his campaign of irritation, just as much as she wondered why he had ever begun it. Life, though peaceful once more, seemed suddenly ordinary, the programme even more lifeless and mundane.

She was relaxing in bed one Sunday evening, when the telephone shrilled.

'Gina?' It was Jimmy. No one else had her private number, which was only to be used in case of emergency. 'Gina, I'm sorry to disturb you, but I've just had a call from one of the sponsors. It seems they're calling a special meeting, tomorrow, early. I wanted to make sure you'd be on time.'

Gina felt unreasonable irritation; he should know she was always punctual for briefings. She had been a businesswoman before she'd become a television personality and, in business, time was money.

'Of course I'll be there,' she said. 'What's it all about?'

'I don't know.' Jimmy sounded uneasy. 'But somehow I sense the winds of change.'

'Change?' Her tone became sharper. 'You don't mean they're thinking of taking the show off or replacing me in the series?' It wouldn't be disaster financially speaking, but it would be a blow to her self-esteem, her belief in her popularity, a setback to ambition.

'I honestly don't know.' Jimmy sounded unhappy. 'I wish I did. But whatever it is, I'll be there, rooting for you.'

'Thanks, and thanks for warning me.' Slowly she replaced the receiver and sank back against frilled, pastel-blue pillowcases. Her mind furiously active, she went over the past two or three shows, seeking for flaws which could have made the sponsors dissatisfied with her. Her fan mail was as steady as ever. The press had been favourable. Was there any significance in the fact that she'd been presenting the show for exactly six months? The current series was ended, and her predecessor had only just completed six months when Gina replaced her ... though *she* had retired voluntarily. The public knew nothing of this. The two girls were sufficiently alike in colouring and stature for the substitution to remain unnoticed. Was there another tall, statuesque redhead somewhere, waiting to step into

Gina's shoes? Ever practical, she bagan to plan ahead
for this contingency. Her own business still awaited her,
ably run by a deputy. She could always go back and
take up the reins once more. Business had proved to be
a panacea before . . .

Unable to return to nursing, Gina had told her
husband she intended to look for another job, but it
had been difficult to find something sufficiently
interesting and stimulating. Then, one day, waiting
patiently in a shop while a foreigner was being served,
the idea was presented to her. Mechanically, she had
noted the price of the item the man bought, simply
because she was about to ask for the same thing. She
was surprised when the figure asked of her was so much
less.

'Surely there must be some mistake?' she'd said, to
find her query treated with callous amusement.

'They've got plenty of money, their sort,' the assistant
told her. 'They can afford to pay more. They don't
quibble.'

'No,' Gina had retorted, unable to contain her
disgust and indignation. 'Because they don't realise
they're being ripped off.'

The more she brooded, the more she disliked this
attitude that overseas visitors were fair game for
overcharging. Out of this sense of indignation grew the
idea of an advisory service for foreigners, whether with
or without a fortune to spend, but with no way of
knowing if they were getting true value. What both
kinds needed was an agent to see they were not cheated.

With the money an elderly aunt had left her and a
personal loan from the bank, Gina had rented a
modest, but centrally situated office. A lot of money
went in advertising, but it paid dividends. Soon it
became known that the GD Agency would get you an
honest deal, would do its best to satisfy any request,
however bizarre. 'We don't claim to perform miracles,

just the next best thing,' was Gina's slogan and it wasn't long before she'd moved to larger premises, taken on several assistants upon whom she impressed her own strict standards of honesty.

Yes, if her television career was about to take a downward swoop, she could always return to business, she thought, as, true to her promise, she arrived promptly at the Television Centre. She had risen early to take more than usual care with her appearance, since there was always the chance that she might be fighting for her job.

Briefly, she took in the presence of several opulent-looking limousines that distinguished the car park by their presence. The 'Big Three' were here. Jimmy's small office was cramped still further by the presence of the three men who were the programme's sponsors. Three? This morning there were four formally suited figures; and, with a sense of outrage, Gina recognised the fourth; her persecutor, Mr X. With a gesture that was instinctive, she threw up her hands to protect her unmasked face, demanding,

'What the hell are *you* doing here?'

There was a pregnant silence, during which she heard the uneasy clearing of throats, and then one of the sponsors, a white-haired, elderly man, was reproving her.

'Miss Darcy! That's no way to address Mr Fallon.'

Fallon? It meant nothing to her. A week or two ago he had been merely another guest on her show. How had he conned his way into the select circle of those who knew her real name?

'Mr Tod Fallon is a new shareholder in TLM Enterprises, a *considerable* shareholder,' he emphasised. 'And since he has never met you, I suggested that he attend this meeting. He has a few questions to ask.'

Oh, yes, Gina thought ironically, Mr Benson might

think the suggestion was his, but she knew who had brainwashed him into making it.

'Actually, Mr Fallon and I *have* met before,' she said coldly. 'Twice. On both occasions, he made a considerable nuisance of himself and made some very insulting suggestions. If Mr Fallon had a financial interest in me, why couldn't he have said so instead of subjecting me to a third degree, just before an important filming session; instead of infiltrating his way on to the show? Doesn't he realise just how long a waiting list there is to appear with Fantasy Woman? And yet he uses his influence to take up a place. Besides, his questions could just as easily have been answered by any of you.' She looked around at the three men and was disconcerted to see that they all looked uneasy.

'I don't think you quite understand, Miss Darcy.' Mr Benson seemed to have elected himself as spokesman. 'Mr Fallon is now the principal shareholder in our firm and as such he has the right to make policy decisions. It's some of these decisions he wants to discuss with you.'

Gina was aghast. For the last year, the trio of elderly men had been content to accept Jimmy's advice, her own suggestions, on the way the programme should develop. She knew there was no way Tod Fallon was going to be so complacent. Fear fluttered in her stomach, a fear she would not show and that made the thrust of her chin more belligerent.

'Well, bully for Mr Fallon,' she said. 'Perhaps he's looking for a new presenter, since he's obviously dissatisfied with the way things are.'

For the first time since her arrival, Tod Fallon spoke. 'Let's say I have certain plans for you, Miss Darcy.'

'What plans?' she demanded. 'Do I have any say in what I'm asked to do?'

'You will be consulted.'

And any objections she might have would be overridden, Gina thought angrily. So far she had remained standing, her body tense with anger. Now she perched herself on the arm of Jimmy's chair, a study in casually insolent indifference, as she consulted her wristwatch.

'Shall we get to the point then?'

Disconcertingly, he was shaking his head.

'My ideas are far too complex for a brief session. Besides, I wish to speak to you alone. I suggest we take a working lunch and then spend the rest of the day discussing the future. *Fantasy Woman* will be off the screen for a while, until certain other plans have been put into execution.'

Gina was stunned, but she was not going to let this man see the extent of her reaction.

'In that case,' she said, 'I think it would be better if you hold this discussion with Mr Riley. He can keep me advised of your "plans".'

'I don't wish to deal with your producer, Miss Darcy.' His icy politeness matched her own. 'I wish to deal with you. Mr Riley accepts that fact and so, I'm afraid, must you.'

Looking with an appeal at Jimmy, she saw the regretful nod of his ginger head, the helpless spread of his hands.

'Very well.' She sought to hide her angry frustration. 'Then I want Jimmy present at our discussion.'

But Tod Fallon was inflexible. He wanted everything his way, she seethed, as she saw the negative movement of the dark head.

'Just you and me, Miss Darcy. Oh, don't worry. Mr Riley won't be adversely affected. It's accepted that he's to remain the producer of the show in any event.'

'Oh, and suppose I refuse to accept your ideas? I'm not just a puppet that you can manipulate.' There had never before been any unpleasantness in her discussions with the sponsors and she could feel the charged surprise of the three elderly men, who had never known her to be anything but charmingly co-operative.

'We'll deal with that problem if and when it arises,' Tod told her. He shot his cuff, consulting the expensive Rolex watch that banded his strong wrist. 'It's too early for lunch, so I suggest we begin over a coffee. I have a premonition that this discussion is going to take longer than I anticipated.'

He sounded edgy, impatient, as though he were not accustomed to having to negotiate. In whatever field he operated, he was probably surrounded by 'yes' men. He was probably used to women, too, deferring to his lightest word, totally bowled over by his male charisma. Well he would find *her* a very different proposition!

Tod had already come to the same conclusion, even before this meeting. This was no auburn-haired equivalent of the dumb blonde. His first glimpse of that strong chin had reinforced Marcha's warning. But he felt only reluctant admiration for her fiery, independent temperament stir within him; and a man would have to be lacking in some way not to appreciate her appearance, which, this morning, was singularly dramatic. He was pretty sure she knew just how effective her outfit was against the cream of her skin, the red glow of her hair. A fine striped, black wool jumpsuit, worn with a red leather belt and red shoes. A red pigskin clutch bag and a stylish black fedora hat, tilted at a defiantly rakish angle, completed the picture. Yes, she was quite something. This was definitely not a woman who could be domineered, and she would require more subtle handling than he had orginally intended to employ. But whatever tactics he had to use, he was determined that the result would be the same in the end. She might be strong, but he was stronger and, something he had not expected, he had a weapon against which, he had already discovered, she was not, after all, immune. Marcha need never know what methods he had employed; the means justified the end, which would be to her benefit.

Gina had been well aware of his scrutiny and she wondered what thoughts were passing through that well-shaped head. Some sixth sense warned her they were thoughts which, in some way, boded her no good.

Suddenly the brief consultation with the other sponsors was over and Gina found herself, Tod's large hand at her elbow, being urged towards the door. Over her shoulder, she cast a glance at Jimmy. His features were drawn into angry lines, but there was also a worried expression in his eyes. By nature, Jimmy was an optimist and that he should so openly show his anxiety added to Gina's own sense of unease. Just what had Tod Fallon got in mind that was going to take so long to discuss? Would she be forced into taking a stand or was there the remotest possibility that his suggestions would be acceptable to her? Bemused by the rapidity of events, she allowed him to usher her into the gleaming, chauffeur-driven Rolls Royce.

An expensive car, and he was expensively dressed. From the corner of her eye, she was conscious of muscular thighs in taut, well-cut dark trousers; the Gucci shoes. His shirt was undoubtedly of pure silk, his tie a discreet statement in slate blue. Her mental catalogue ended as her eyes lifted further, to his face, and met a brooding black gaze intent upon her. He had been fully aware of her comprehensive assessment. Unconsciously, her chin lifted.

'Where are we going?'

'My hotel.'

'Oh! I thought you had an office. Isn't a hotel rather a public place?' Especially, she thought, since their discussion might well become acrimonious.

'I don't have an office in London. But I do have a suite at the hotel. I think that will ensure us complete privacy, if that's what you have in mind.' A quizzical, sideways glance caught her face creased into an expression of doubt. In the last year, the only man with whom she'd been completely alone was Jimmy Riley and he didn't present any threat to her composure, as she knew, from the other night, this man did.

'Unless you'd rather we went to your place? I assume *you* live in London?'

'No!' she snapped, then, 'I mean, yes, I do have a flat in London, but no, we're not going there.'

'Private love nest is it?' His deep, incisive voice mocked her.

'It's private,' she agreed levelly, 'but nothing else.'

'What?' He was openly incredulous. 'No "Mr Fantasy"?'

'Mr Fallon,' she said icily, 'I'm perfectly prepared to answer your questions where they concern my work. My private life is not for discussion.'

The laugh that greeted her remark was a short, cynical bark.

'That means no man! If there had been, you'd have been only too ready to claim his existence.'

'Why should I need, or want, to lie about a thing like that?'

'Pride?' he conjectured. 'No woman likes to admit that she hasn't got a man in tow.'

'But then, perhaps I'm different to the other women you know, Mr Fallon.'

His glance assessed her, very comprehensively.

'Oh no!' he drawled insinuatingly. 'I don't think so.'

She could feel the angry colour rising, was furious that she couldn't control or hide it. Though the width of the seat was between them, she was unwillingly aware of his overpowering virility and his look had been blatantly sexual in its implications.

Against her will, she was impressed by his suite; that he was used to such a lifestyle was evident in his casual ease, the way in which he summoned room service, ordered coffee and announced that his guest would be staying for lunch. Invited to sit down, Gina sank into the luxury of a settee upholstered in a soft pile, cream velvet, but wished she had chosen an armchair when he joined her.

'Tell me, Miss Darcy, are you totally satisfied with your screen image?'

'Not totally,' she admitted slowly. 'I love meeting people, satisfying their ambitions. That part's fine.'

'Then in what way *are* you dissatisfied?' He was watching her all the time he spoke, as if he were taking face and figure item by item, assessing all the component parts that made up Gina Darcy, and she turned her head aside, made half annoyed, half self-conscious by his scrutiny.

'I'm not keen on the mask, the loss of my identity.'

'Aah!' It was difficult to interpret the sound. 'Tell me more.' Was he trying to trap her into an expression of displeasure; looking for some reason to replace her?

'I'd rather you told me just what you have in mind,' Gina said, still deliberately not looking at him. 'That's why we're here.' But he was not to be diverted.

'It's part and parcel of the same thing. So, the mask?'

'All right! I don't go for the incognito approach, but the sponsors wanted it, so . . . *I* want my face to be seen and recognised. I'm ambitious, Mr Fallon. I don't believe the show's popular *because* of my anonymity. It would be just as successful, perhaps more, if the viewers could see me. Like you,' she added resentfully, 'half of them probably think I'm disfigured.'

'Except that now *I* know that's not so, but very much the opposite.' To her alarm, a strong hand captured her chin and forced her to face him. For a moment his voice had been caressive, than it snapped back into interrogative mood. 'So you want to be famous? Fame can be a chancy thing.'

'It was pure chance that got me into television in the first place, plus experience in providing people with what they wanted.' She wasn't going to volunteer any further information, matters which didn't concern Tod Fallon, matters which included the failure of her marriage.

Tod watched as she brooded. He knew a fair bit about her past, mainly from Marcha. By all accounts, Gina Darcy was a hard-headed woman, selfish, not one to take a back seat, which was going to make his task that much harder—not initially, but later, when he had to reveal the full extent of his plans.

'Drink your coffee,' he urged.

The coffee smelt delicious, but Gina was more interested in the answer to certain questions.

'According to Mr Benson, you're the principal shareholder in TLM Enterprises, so why have we never met officially?' She flushed hectically as she recalled the nature of their second informal encounter.

'I've only become a shareholder in the last month. We may not have met "officially", but I've been making a close study of you.'

'Why?' Gina asked suspiciously. 'Aren't you satisfied with my work?'

'Not entirely.' This was blunt. Tod Fallon certainly didn't believe in pulling his punches. But Gina wasn't going to show him that this one had struck below the belt. 'Certain changes will have to be made.'

She kept her voice level, purposely unconcerned.

'Does that include replacing me?'

CHAPTER THREE

'THAT depends on whether you're prepared to co-operate.' Tod was aware that he was bluffing. Suppose she called his bluff? Mentally, he crossed his fingers. If Gina proved recalcitrant, it could take him a long time to find another woman anywhere near as suitable.

'Co-operate?' she murmured non-committally.

'Don't sound so suspicious.' His dark eyes mocked her fears. Again he reached out one large, bronzed hand to grasp her chin, and she had to force herself to meet his gaze as he made an itemised study of her features.

'Great green cat's eyes,' he mused, 'and red hair. An inflammable combination. Redheads are reputed to be quick-tempered, as are cats, and I think I've already seen the flash of your claws.' With interest, he watched the colour flood her lovely face.

'Could we confine our discussion to business?' she asked coldly, trying to ignore the feelings the warmth of his hand was producing. As he had intended, she had a sudden terrifying image of Tod Fallon making love to her on this sofa. What kind of subconscious tricks was her mind playing? Or was it her mind? She was a normal, healthy young woman; except for one thing, she thought bitterly, and for a long time she had been suppressing normal urges. No, that wasn't quite right. The urges hadn't been there. But now . . .

'Did you know that your nose has the most delightful sprinkling of freckles?' he continued, as if he hadn't heard her demand.

'I know my failings!' she snapped, very much afraid that soon, if he didn't release her, loss of control would be one of them.

'Failings?' He repeated the word thoughtfully. 'The freckles? Oh no, they give you a reassuring touch of humanity. Too much perfection can be rather frightening. But then,' he added softly, 'you're far from perfect, aren't you?'

'What do you mean?' Gina tried to jerk away from him, but Tod's fingers had a vice like hold of her. He couldn't possibly know about . . .

'Oh, I'm not referring to your physical attributes.' His dark eyes were bold as they swept downward from her face over other, more concealed, yet still apparent aspects of her femininity; and an outraged Gina could read his mind. It was quite beside the point that, a moment or two ago, she had been imagining much the same thing; but his words had broken the spell.

Tod, too, had been surprised at the trend of his own thoughts. Whatever kind of co-operation he hoped to wring from Gina Darcy, it wasn't that kind. His idea had been to flatter her, to seduce her into agreement with his plan; seduction of a metaphorical, not a literal nature. But, damn it, he was a man wasn't he? Just because he was committed to one woman it didn't mean he couldn't appreciate the rest of the species. Outwardly, Gina Darcy was something quite spectacular, even if he didn't much like what he'd been told about her character.

'Just what *are* you referring to?' she demanded.

He prevaricated. He had no wish for Gina to learn how much he knew about her. Not unnaturally she would be curious about his sources of information and that was something he was not yet ready to divulge.

'Whatever contributed to the break-up of your marriage. That would suggest failings of some kind. Your marriage didn't last very long.'

She gasped. Still, she shouldn't be surprised. Tod Fallon was the kind of man who would make it his business to know all about anyone on his payroll.

'That's past history,' she snapped. 'Something I prefer to forget.'

'Maybe. But it's all part of you, made you what you are. Tell me, why *did* you divorce your husband?'

'You mean,' sarcastically, 'there's something you don't know?'

'I've heard one version,' coolly, 'but I'd be curious to hear yours.'

'Well, you won't. It's none of your business.'

'Oh no, Miss Darcy. You're wrong! From now on, everything about you is my business.'

Their eyes met. His were so dark that the pupils were indistinguishable from the velvety irises; it was as if she were being drawn into the depths. Her expression must have changed, revealing her awareness of him, for he smiled slowly, that lop-sided, attractive smile which made such an alteration to his normally grave face. Something, somewhere deep inside her, leapt wildly. Oddly breathless, she gave him back look for look.

What on earth was the matter with her? She didn't like Tod Fallon. She didn't trust him. She'd known from the very beginning that there was an element of danger in his acquaintance. From their very first encounter he seemed to have gone out of his way, sometimes to taunt and insult her, sometimes to flatter, insinuatively, almost seductively. Why? And yet, against her will, there was something about him that drew her.

After Keith, she'd sworn that no man would ever have the chance to come near her, mentally or physically, to affect her pulse rate; but Tod seemed to have achieved all of these things, insidiously, but surely. Yet she felt certain he'd had no intention of doing so. He seemed to like her as little as she liked him; and that was another puzzle. Apart from their brief, previous clashes, she had done nothing to earn his censure. But it was almost as if he disapproved of her. Was it her work, or her personality?

'Were you ever in love with your husband?' His voice broke her trance-like state.

'Of course, when I married him,' she said curtly, still unwilling to discuss her private affairs. It seemed to her that the more knowledge he had of her, the more power he could exercise over her.

'And afterwards, before the divorce?'

'No. He'd succeeded by that time in killing every vestige of feeling I'd ever had for him.' She shivered as she remembered that claustrophobic possessiveness and jealousy, but most of all, how he had finally destroyed her.

Tod was surprised at the curiosity he felt about Gina and her husband. It had nothing to do with him, nor with their future association. Probably it was because she was such a damned attractive woman that he wanted to hear her deny what he'd been told, convince him that she had not been the one at fault.

'So you put all the blame on him, then?' His enquiring tone sounded derogatory, accusing, to Gina's over-sensitive ear.

'No!' she said and saw that she'd surprised him. 'I know my ambitions contributed to our break-up. Keith was bitterly jealous of my work, my friends. He wanted a *Hausfrau* running after him, feeding him, doing his washing and ironing, and it just wasn't me.'

'Is that all he required?' Tod asked in an insinuative tone that made her flush. 'Surely there were *some* fringe benefits?'

'There's more to love and marriage,' she retorted, 'than good sex and a few shared tastes. There has to be trust. If you want to hold someone, then you also have to know when to let go.' Then, with a return of her indignation, 'I don't know why I'm telling *you* all this.'

'Because I have my reasons for needing to know. And has there been anyone else since?' He went on inexorably with his catechism.

'No, Mr Fallon, there has not! And I don't intend
that there will be. I discovered that marriage and a
career don't mix, so I've settled for the career, freedom,
independence.'

'A very suitable frame of mind for what I intend for
you; no distracting relationships. But then, I wasn't
necessarily implying marriage when I asked if there was
anyone else.'

Her green eyes snapped at him, matching her tone of
voice.

'I don't know what standards *you* hold, Mr Fallon,
but *I* don't go in for "casual" relationships.'

Considering what he'd been told of her, Tod was
surprised at her total honesty. He'd expected her to
refute any faults on her own part, any responsibility for
the failure of her marriage. But then he was almost
constantly revising his preconceived ideas about
Fantasy Woman. As to a career versus marriage, he had
no doubt she meant what she said right at this moment.
But there was always the chance that some man would
persuade her otherwise.

He wondered, as he had done before, whether it
would be safer for his purposes to ensure her co-
operation by making her fall in love with *him*. He had
no doubt of his ability to do so, and it would serve to
bind her to him for the necessary length of time.

Yet, despite this deliberately cold calculation, he
knew that the physical attraction he felt towards her
was genuine. She was extraordinarily lovely; tall,
statuesque, no, almost Junoesque in her build. Both
body and face held a passionate promise of generosity
for any man who could penetrate the icy shell she had
constructed around her heart.

That her mouth could be ardent, he already knew. It
was a large mouth, and it should have been ugly. Yet,
because of its flawless shape, it wasn't. Unbidden there
came to him an acute physical remembrance of that

mouth's unwilling response. He'd seen the alarm in her
eyes, too, wide set, a shade of green he didn't recall
encountering before, when she'd thought he was about
to touch her. So she hadn't forgotten, either, the
chemistry that momentarily had flowed between them.

But might it not be dangerous for him to attempt to
tamper with her affections? Could he risk personal
involvement this time, now that he and Marcha ...
Perhaps he would do better to stick to a straightforward
business proposition, and in surroundings where the
attraction he felt had to be disguised. Wiser, yes. But he
still felt a sense of disappointment.

'I don't intend to renew your contract for *Fantasy
Woman* just for the present,' he said, deliberately brisk.

She stared at him. His decision must already have
been made, so why the pretence at discussion? Why
wait until now, when her fears of just such an
eventuality had begun to abate somewhat?

'Why?' It was ridiculous the way her voice quivered.
'Have you found someone to replace me?' Her thought
processes were swift and her eyes narrowed. '*That's*
why you've bought your way into TLM Enterprises, so
you can keep some girlfriend of yours sweet.'

It was uncomfortably close to the truth, but, 'Not at
all!' His manner was annoyingly laconic. She had hoped
to see her shot go home, see anger stir his imperturbable
surface. 'Correct me if I'm wrong, but I believe you did
express a wish to test out the stunts performed on the
show? Gina, it was Jimmy who held you back, not the
sponsors. They're quite willing for you to take a more
active part in the show, provided ...' He paused quite
deliberately, as he studied her lovely face for its
reaction; and it was there, the eager flicker of
anticipation he'd hoped to see. 'Provided you put
yourself entirely in my hands for the next six months.'

She quailed at the thought, but this time she was
able to hide her feelings.

'And what happens to the show meanwhile?' she demanded.

'It goes on, of course, with a substitute.'

'I knew it!' She began to rise from the table. 'You *are* putting in some girlfriend . . .'

'Shut up! Sit down and listen. I've no idea *who* they'll use and frankly I don't give a damn. That's your Jimmy's problem.'

She regarded him steadily for a few moments. Maybe he was speaking the truth, maybe not.

'And what will *we* be doing during that six months?'

'*You*,' he emphasised, 'if you agree, will be putting in some pretty strict training to become a stunt girl. In fact, if you're the right material, by the time I've finished with you, you may not want to return to something as tame as *Fantasy Woman*.'

He watched as realisation flooded her lovely face, as incredulity, dawning hope, radiant excitement followed each other in quick succession.

'You really mean it?'

'Yes.'

'When do I start?'

'You're not afraid?'

'No way.'

'Right,' he said, unable to conceal his satisfaction. 'Can you be ready by Saturday?'

'Of course! But ready for what, and where?'

'In the first instance you'll come down to Mallions, my home. A great deal of your training can take place there and in the immediate neighbourhood. Most of the necessary facilities are available.'

'No!' Gina protested at once. 'I can't come and stay with you, just like that. What about my flat? I'd rather do my training nearer home.' Tod Fallon would have to accept that she had a mind and will of her own. Somehow the thought of several months on his territory, the advantage inevitably his, worried her.

'You can't.' He was inexorable. 'There are no comparable facilities. Besides, I intend to keep a personal eye on your training; and there are other reasons why I have to work from home.' He gave her no further chance to argue, but rose from his seat. 'Right! That's settled, I'll drive you home.'

'No!' she said again; then, catching his lowering expression, 'thank you, but I prefer to take a taxi.'

He said nothing for a moment as she met his eyes defiantly. She thought he was going to insist, but, instead, he shrugged and felt in his inside pocket for a pen.

'Then you'd better give me your address, so I know where to pick you up on Saturday.'

'I'm sorry. I don't give my address to anyone. If you'll set a time, I'll meet you here, or anywhere else convenient to you. Now, if you'll excuse me, I believe I saw a taxi rank outside?'

Tod fought his exasperation. He couldn't remember when he'd ever met a woman so stubbornly determined to go her own way, except Marcha, of course, but hers was a special case. Still, he had gained the initial advantage. Gina had accepted his challenge and once she was actually on his territory, he would reveal the further extent of his plans. There were other ways of discovering what he wanted to know right now.

'I'll see you to your taxi then. Can you be here by ten o'clock Saturday morning?'

'Of course.' She was so relieved by his easy acquiescence that she would have promised to be there at six, if he'd suggested it.

The taxi rank was only a hundred yards from the hotel, but Tod was punctilious in seeing Gina into the first vehicle. She had been careful, he noted with dry amusement, to refrain from giving the driver her direction before he pulled away from the kerb. Casually, Tod strolled back towards the next cab in line and, before Gina's taxi was out of sight, he was offering the driver double fare if he could succeed in following her, unobserved.

Gina sank back into a chair. Thank heaven Todd had not insisted on accompanying her home. What did she really think of him? What really disconcerted her was his habit of staring at her. One moment it was as if he 'fancied' her, the next as though his plans for her boded no good. Which was the real Tod Fallon?

As the flat's soothing ambience closed around her, Gina wondered whether she could bear to leave its familiar security for a whole six months. Though she'd agreed to the training Todd had suggested she had no idea what particular skills he would ask of her, nor if she would prove capable of mastering them. He hadn't even enquired about her athletic prowess. She might have been able to surprise him by her list of accomplishments.

Nevertheless, she was grateful for Tod Fallon's intervention at this stage in her career. With more skills to offer, other areas of the media might open up to her, fields requiring more than a pretty face and a desirable body, which could not last forever. Right now, though, that body was badly in need of the soothing relaxation of warm water.

Later, wandering through to the bedroom, wrapped toga-wise in a large bath sheet, she sat on the edge of the bed and, from the bedside cabinet, took out a photograph album. Flicking over the earlier years, she paused to study herself as she had been at nineteen, when she'd first met Keith. She was better looking now, and her brain was more informed. But at twenty-five she might be said to have reached her peak of attraction. How much longer would she go on looking like this? How much longer before she had to really *work* at being attractive?

It was a relief to have these depressing thoughts interrupted, until she realised just what the source of the interruption was: the doorbell.

Damn! She'd hoped that none of her neighbours had witnessed her return. Without being uncivil, Gina had firmly discouraged casual droppings in; but there was one elderly woman who could not be dissuaded from borrowing the occasional half-pint of milk and as meticulously returning it.

Sighing resignedly, she discarded the bath sheet in favour of a silk wrap and headed for the source of the irritation. Obviously it was no use pretending she wasn't in.

Tod paid off his taxi, but with the success of his tailing operation, he lost his impetus. For a while he walked up and down outside the apartment block, imagining Gina's reaction when she opened the door and saw him. He had no doubts of his ability to gain entry. He would have the advantage of being prepared for the confrontation and he was physically stronger. It would be a confrontation. She would be furious, of course.

Hell! Was he afraid of her? With an impatient shrug, he swung in through the double front doors, pausing momentarily to study the names against the apartment numbers. His eyebrows rose as he saw she was on the top floor, in the penthouse, no less.

Why go any further, he wondered. He had her address; that was all he needed. He knew why. He was curious about Gina, the private woman, her background. He wanted to see her with her defences down. As the lift carried him upward, he felt the sudden unexpected warmth of sensuality engulf him at the thought of being alone with Gina in her apartment. Good God! What was he thinking of? What would Marcha think if she could read his mind at this moment?

Outside Gina's door, he took himself to task. It was weakness to let such emotions ride him. His use of his masculinity must be calculated, with no danger of serious involvement on his part.

She opened the door, recoiled, the polite smile freezing into a grimace of angry horror.

'What the hell are *you* doing here? How did you find out where I live?'

'Easy!' Tod crossed the threshold, brushing past her with as much nonchalance as if he had been invited to do so. 'I followed you.'

'Damn you! How dare you!' Gina's words drifted after Tod's back view, and she felt a sense of ridiculous anti-climax as he preceded her into her living-room, threw himself down on to *her* favourite seat.

'I thought,' he said, as he looked around him with a calm appraisal that infuriated her, 'in view of our new policy, your secretiveness about your address was a little outmoded.'

'Oh?' she snapped. 'And do you intend to publicise that? So that the world and his wife can swarm all over my doorstep, invade my privacy?'

'No,' he drawled. 'This is a privilege I intend to reserve for myself, assuming I am the first man to cross your hallowed threshold?'

She refused to give him the satisfaction of acknowledging or denying his words.

'Right! So you've got what you wanted. You know where I live. Now you can get out!' Dramatically, she pointed towards the door, the dignity of the gesture impaired as she realised that the silky, material belt had come unfastened, so that she was forced to grab the edges of her robe and clasp it more firmly about her slim waist.

Apart from a lop-sided smile that recognised her predicament, Tod made no indication of having heard her words. Instead he rose and strolled casually through

the apartment, looking speculatively about him. He
even had the colossal nerve, Gina seethed, to inspect
her bedroom. What did he expect to learn from that?
Was he looking for traces of male occupation? And
what did that matter to him?

'Hmm! You have good taste, *expensive* taste.'

'I've worked damned hard for what I have,' she said
defensively, and, seeing that he had no immediate
intention of leaving, she shot into the hallway and
slammed the apartment door.

'Not furnished on hefty alimony payments then?' His
gesture encompassed the décor, the antiques, the
Impressionist paintings.

'No!' she snapped. 'It isn't.'

When her marriage had finally broken up, she'd
refused alimony; she wanted nothing from Keith. She
didn't need his money. Her agency was prospering and
there was no reason why it shouldn't go on doing so.
But even if she'd been on the breadline, it would have
sickened her to be dependent on Keith.

'You were the guilty party, perhaps?' Tod suggested.

'I most certainly was not!' Her green eyes blazed fire
at him at the injustice of the remark.

'*He* was unfaithful to *you*?' Tod's incredulity
stemmed from the thought that, if such were the case,
her husband must have been all kinds of a damned fool
not to know the treasure he'd had in his possession.

'Yes,' Gina confirmed dully. She sat down in the
cushioned recess. Since Tod seemed unlikely to depart
until he had finally satisfied his curiosity, she might as
well be comfortable.

'Tell me,' Tod suggested, joining her uninvited, his
proximity disturbingly unwelcome. Imperceptibly she
tried to edge away.

She shook her auburn head. She had never related
the exact details of that traumatic time to anyone.

'Perhaps your marriage was never consummated,' he

insinuated. 'If you behaved like this, like a frightened virgin, every time your husband came near you, I'm not surprised he looked elsewhere.'

'Never consummated!' She knew her voice sounded shrill, orchestrated by indignation, a sudden stab of pure physical frustration. How dared Tod Fallon, a total stranger until a few hours ago, make such an outrageous insinuation! Keith, far from being deprived, had had his cake *and* eaten it.

'Before I met you,' Todd informed her, 'someone told me your marriage failed, not only because you were highly ambitious, but also because you were frigid.'

'Then that "someone" is a liar!' She faced him squarely, her green eyes angry but steady. Who could have told him such a thing? She shook her head vehemently, the movement making the gleaming red hair swirl about her silk-clad shoulders, its perfume drifting to Tod's nostrils a heady enticement, and a wave of pure eroticism shafted through him as he felt himself wishing that he might be the one to put her to the test.

'Care to prove that to me?' he heard himself saying softly. His eyes held hers and hers were the first to drop.

'Get out!' she muttered. She was trembling with a sudden anguished desire that his words had aroused. It had been so long since she'd known a man's touch, the exploration of his hands upon her body, a man's lovemaking. She'd managed to quell the need for so long, but now it rose in a flood tide that threatened to engulf her, because she *knew* Tod Fallon was capable of assuaging that need. He was the only man who had managed to penetrate her reserve, to give new life to senses she'd believed permanently frozen, the only man to move her physically in a long, long time.

'I don't think you mean that.' He was too perceptive. He leant towards her, slowly, tantalisingly, and she seemed incapable of movement, of retreat.

CHAPTER FOUR

THERE was a brief second when his mouth was only a butterfly touch on hers, when there was still time for her to retreat. But she hesitated an instant too long. Then Tod's weight carried her back full-length upon the settee, his kiss deepening as the hardness of his chest crushed her soft breasts.

All along Gina had known instinctively that this man represented danger and she had realised the form that danger took. She should be fighting him off, she thought bemusedly, but her body, so long controlled, had betrayed her. Scarcely knowing what she did, she moved beneath him, a deep, primitive sound vibrating in her throat.

Without removing his lips from hers, he levered himself a little away, so that his hand might invade the scanty protection of her silken robe, might have access between their bodies to the fullness of her breasts. She couldn't move. She knew what he wanted to do, knew she wanted it, too. His hand found the smooth flesh he sought. He raised his head, so that his eyes could devour what he had discovered, the darkening aureole, the hardening tips of her breasts. He lowered his head again, not to her lips this time, but to those rosy tips, the movement of his tongue, his teeth, imparting an ecstasy part pleasure, part pain.

'Oh please, please, don't!' she heard herself saying, knew that while her mind was still coherent, her body was not.

'You don't mean that,' he murmured.

'I do . . . I don't want . . .'

'Nonsense! You told the truth, Gina. You're *not*

frigid. You're no unawakened virgin; you've been
married. You're a mature, sexually attractive woman,
and you've been starving yourself of love. You want
me.'

Yes, she thought miserably, the first time in years I've
allowed myself to want a man and it had to be *you*, a
man I hardly know and dare not trust.

But even these thoughts could not stem the primitive
flood of awareness surging through her as, against her
will, her body responded to the proximity of his, its
muscular hardness, its musky scent. She was coming
dangerously close to forgetting her self-imposed tenets
of behaviour where men were concerned.

He had succeeded now in sliding the robe from her
shoulders and as it fell in a silken pool around her hips,
she heard him exclaim beneath his breath, knew his
wondering gaze was roaming lingeringly over her naked
curves. An exploratory hand began to stroke her skin,
the intimate lingering of his fingers triggering off sharp
sensations deep within her.

'You're very lovely, Gina.' His voice was husky,
shaken. He took her mouth again and this time she
found her lips parting, responding willingly to his
probing, moist invasion. His fingers tightened their
grasp of her; his mouth trailed its burning route down
the side of her neck, pausing tantalisingly at her nipples,
to encompass, to stimulate, then on down the flat curve
of her stomach to the indentation of her navel. The
warmth of pleasure heated her loins and yet . . .

'Tod! Please!' Somewhere she found sufficient breath
to make the protest she knew she ought to make.

'Please what? Please make love to you?'

'No! Ah! No!' She wanted him. How she wanted him!
But not like this. She didn't know anything about him.
If she were ever again to be intimate with a man, first
she must know him through and through, be certain
that he was worthy of her admiration and trust, as well

as her love. Without that knowledge there could be no
self-respect in her giving.

Frantically she pushed him away. Amazingly he did
not resist. Instead he rose to stand over her, his eyes
clouded, remote, as he watched her trembling fingers
attempt to straighten the silk robe.

'Don't worry, Gina. I didn't intend to go all the way.'

'You never stood a chance of doing so!' she retorted,
the shame at the liberties she had allowed now
overwhelming her.

'No?' Despite his own self-disgust, he raised a
satirical eyebrow. 'Allow me to differ.'

She jumped to her feet, the fiery temper that went
with her hair aroused by his arrogant presumption.

'You can think what you like! You can't possibly
know what I think or feel, so I'll tell you. I think
you're despicable. Just because you've bought your way
into TLM, into *Fantasy Woman*, doesn't mean you've
bought me, too. If I agree to work with you . . .'

'If?' he enquired sardonically, 'I seem to remember
you leaping at my offer.'

'I can still change my mind!' she flared. 'And if
there's any repetition of . . . your . . . your behaviour, I
will change it. Just remember, *if* I still agree to work
with you, that's the only kind of co-operation you can
expect.'

But that was all he wanted, wasn't it, Tod asked
himself as he, too, rose, making her a sardonic half-bow
of acknowledgement. He already knew she was eager
and willing to take part in his new venture, so why had
he still thought it necessary to try the ploy of binding
her closer to him by the mutual attraction he knew
existed? Always honest with himself, at least, Tod knew
that for those few minutes no such devious considera-
tions had been in his mind. The plain fact of the matter
was that he had desired her, desired her desperately.
For God's sake, what had got into him? Usually clear

thinking, master of his own moods, Tod didn't relish
bewilderment at his own motives. He must be missing
Marcha, he decided. He'd been too long away from her.

'My humble apologies!' he said, aware that he
sounded far from humble, aware that he was inflaming
her irritation. 'I was under the impression that you
weren't averse to being kissed.'

'That's a typical male attitude!' She was scornful
now. 'To imagine that just because a woman doesn't
have some one currently dancing attendance, she'll be
pathetically grateful for any man's attention.'

Tod didn't like allowing a woman to have the last
word, but, prudently, he recognised that Gina was very
different from most women of his acquaintance. Having
secured her agreement to work with him, there was no
point in alienating her. He must keep his prime
objective to the forefront of his mind. He moved
towards the door.

'Until Saturday then,' he said, his tone now matter-
of-fact. Then, with a brief flash of mischievousness, 'I
presume there's no objection to my calling for you here,
now I've discovered your hideout?'

After his departure, Gina made no attempt to dress.
She didn't feel she had the strength. Instead, she sank
back on to the cushions that still bore the impression of
their combined weight.

She could scarcely believe in the happenings of the
last half hour. She realised that in some subtle way Tod
Fallon was not really interested in her as a woman, but
as a commodity. And why, when she'd resisted the
efforts of so many men, had she failed to resist Tod?
For, despite her wariness where he was concerned, she
couldn't deny her growing fascination.

But worse than the knowledge of her failure to
hold out against him, was the recognition of the
nature of the ache that had begun to grow within her,
like the thawing of some great glacier, not only in his

presence, but just at the thought of him; and it frightened her.

Despairingly, she looked around her, but for the first time the quiet peace of her flat did not appeal. Tod Fallon had only entered it once and yet he had left an indelible imprint. The old, cosy feeling of being in an impregnable haven, listening to the external, alien noises, had gone. Suddenly silence didn't appeal any more and she rose to put on a record. She felt lonely, a sensation she hadn't experienced in a long time, and angry with herself for feeling that way, and she had a strong suspicion as to the identity of the responsible catalyst.

Damn it! She was getting maudlin. Men, marriage, were not for her ever again. It was a long time since she'd taken out the failure of her marriage and really looked at it. That she'd done so lately was entirely Tod Fallon's fault. Until just recently she'd been so certain that personal freedom was preferable to the restrictions of a close relationship. But what if it hadn't been marriage itself that was at fault? Suppose it had been the participants. Not just Keith, but her, too. What if she had never really been in love, since so many little issues had annoyed her, including curtailment of her personal liberty.

Keith hadn't liked Gina's success. His pride demanded that he be the dominant partner, the breadwinner, whereas Gina's independent spirit needed equality. She wanted a loving relationship, but it must also allow her to retain originality of thought and action. Most of all Keith had disliked her work bringing her into contact with other attractive, wealthy men. His so-called love, his fear of losing her, had been suffocating. His moods, heralded by brooding, sullen preoccupation, could, at a moment's notice, flare into noisy, unreasonable accusation. He had believed her career to be a 'whim', that eventually she must and would conform to his ideas, but, on the contrary, her work had absorbed more and more of her time and energy. Yet she had genuinely believed she could cope with career and marriage.

Keith's work continually took *him* away from home and he didn't seem to consider that made him any less of an asset as a husband. Why should a career adversely affect her value as a wife? She'd tried every way she knew to cure him of his emotional jealousy, continually reassuring him of her constancy. She'd even begged him to go with her to a Marriage Guidance Councillor, or to see a psychiatrist, but in vain.

They'd been married two years when Keith presented his ultimatum. Either she settled down to being a full-time wife or their marriage was at an end. It forced her to sit down and take stock. Even if theirs wasn't a good relationship, she believed in the marriage vows she'd taken. But she did love her challenging career, was proud of the success she'd made of her agency. She suggested a compromise. She would do as he asked, employ a manager, if they could start a family. To her indignant amazement, Keith refused. He didn't want any encumbrances; to share her attention. It seemed to Gina that he wanted everything his own way.

A couple of months later, fate intervened. After a particularly lively New Year party, they had forgotten to take precautions. Gina was pregnant. Perhaps, she thought, Keith wouldn't mind too much. Her optimism was short-lived. He even refused to believe that the child was his.

It had never occurred to Gina that Keith's displays of jealousy had been a disguise for his own desire for outside sexual experience. His accusations that she was having an affair had been a cover for his own liaison. Gina might never have known of this if Frances hadn't come to see her. Keith didn't know of her visit, but

Gina must let him have a divorce, because she, Frances, was pregnant and Keith must marry her.

It was inevitable that Gina had begun to compare Tod with Keith. Had Keith ever made her feel the heat of sexual desire that she felt flooding through her now, as she remembered Tod's hands upon her naked breasts, his lips hot and seeking on hers? Would Tod really have called a halt if she had not?

From this point, her thoughts turned to the future, to her next encounter with Tod. How should she face him, with this recent incident lying between them? Coolly, that was the answer, on her guard at all times. He must never guess how much he had affected her. She must keep before him her determination that their relationship would be strictly that of business.

It was going to be difficult. If she hadn't wanted this opportunity to further her career, she would have taken the coward's way out and made sure they never met again.

'I imagine you're accustomed to flying? You'll have flown quite a bit on location work?'

Tod had been making most of the conversation since he'd picked Gina up at her flat; none of it, to her relief, of a personal nature.

'Actually, no. I've only been in a plane once in my life.' Gina hoped her face hadn't paled. She wasn't going to admit to Tod that there was anything that scared her, that he had picked on her Achilles' heel. But during the flight in question she had been literally paralysed with fear which, despite all her attempts at rationalisation, she had been unable to conquer. Since then, programmes that involved filming overseas had been made by the camera team and Gina had merely introduced them from the studio.

'Oh?' Tod sounded mildly surprised. 'It doesn't make any difference, except that I wondered if you were troubled by airsickness at all?'

'We'll be going abroad by plane?' If she had to
spend any length of time in the air, with him at her
side, there was no way she'd be able to hide her fears.
Not a good recommendation for a stuntgirl! The
answer to her question nearly destroyed her self-
control.

'No. We're not going abroad. But one of the things
you'll have to do is fly a small plane . . . solo!'

Gina felt her stomach flip, her throat close up. They
hadn't discussed the nature of the stunts she would be
expected to perform.

'Why?' she croaked, hastily turned the croak into a
cough, as if something had irritated her throat.

'You'll find out,' was his maddeningly cryptic reply.
He angled a glance at her set face. 'You have some
objection?'

'N . . . no,' she managed. 'Wh . . . why should I?'

'No reason that I can think of. Good. Then a
fortnight's intensive training should be sufficient for
that particular incident.' He drove on towards their
destination, which she now knew to be just north of
Aylesbury in Buckinghamshire.

'Mallions!' Tod said about an hour later, an hour
during which Gina had feigned sleep. But she hadn't
slept. She'd spent the time in appalled contemplation of
what was in store for her, a prospect as daunting as that
of hiding her reactions to Tod himself, the ordeal she
must face without revealing her abject terror. Hiding
her fear was one thing, but how was she to overcome it?
She could only hope that she would be lucky enough to
get an instructor who would be understanding and able
to reassure her.

She opened her eyes. The car had halted before
massive iron gates set in a high wall that seemed to
stretch for ever in either direction. The gates were
locked and two formidably large men, whom Tod

hailed as Greg and Andy, emerged from a gatehouse to
allow the vehicle access.

Once through the gate, the car negotiated a slight
bend in the drive, which straightened out to reveal a
panoramic view of a Tudor house of stately home
proportions, standing in what appeared to be a great
many acres of land.

The instant the Rolls came to a halt before the house,
figures appeared, as if from nowhere; one man to drive
the car away, two more to carry suitcases, while an
elderly woman stood in the doorway to greet them;
Gina realised that she was not family, but the
housekeeper.

'Welcome home, Mr Fallon. I hope you had a
pleasant journey?' and, to Gina, 'Good afternoon, miss.
Your room is ready, but perhaps you'd like some tea
first?'

Gina nodded and smiled her acknowledgement.

'Tea in the library then, Mrs Bush,' Tod requested
briskly. 'Then perhaps you'll be good enough to show
Miss Darcy the general layout of the house. I have an
important phone call to make.'

About to turn away, the housekeeper hesitated.

'Will you be wanting to see Miss Melanie just yet,
sir?'

'No,' Tod said, a little brusquely Gina thought,
wondering who Melanie was that she could be so lightly
dismissed. 'Later will do.'

Tod ushered Gina into the library. From floor to
ceiling, two walls were lined with exquisitely bound
books. Gina wondered cynically whether Tod had ever
read any of them, or whether they were just part of the
décor. He didn't strike her as the kind of man who
could ever sit still long enough to read a book.

The rest of the room was sparsely, though
expensively, furnished. Two large leather chesterfields
faced each other before a massive hearth and a large

leather-topped desk was angled to the fourth wall. This was composed almost entirely of a large mullioned window, looking out over sweeping parkland to the rear of the house. Beyond and above a colourful shrubbery, Gina caught sight of an object, which rose and fell with the breeze. A windsock? She turned to Tod with a question on her lips.

'Yes. That's an airstrip. I have a small Cessna for my private use, the one you'll be learning to fly.'

An insidious suspicion crossed Gina's mind. 'Who's going to teach me?'

'I shall, of course!' His reply confirmed her uneasy conjecture.

The arrival of Mrs Bush with a tray interrupted this topic and, as she sipped her tea, Gina avoided any return to it by complimenting Tod on his house.

'Has it been in your family long?' she asked, as she studied a large oil painting hung above the fireplace. The work depicted a beruffed Elizabethan gentleman in doublet and hose.

Tod smiled, that brief flash of white teeth which lent his face such disconcerting charm.

'Sorry to disappoint you, but I can't claim any lengthy noble descent. I bought the place lock, stock and barrel, including the family portraits, about five years ago when the last member of the family died.' Again that glimmer of amusement. 'Now you're here, you'll find out a lot about me you didn't know. Perhaps,'—the gleam in his eye, its suspect implication, disconcerted her—'the reverse will apply and I'll be finding out more about you. What else would you like to know?'

'Nothing,' she said sharply, 'I wasn't prying.'

'Nonetheless, I'll give you a brief résumé; it will save explanations later. Tod Fallon, christened Theodore, which incidentally I hate! Age, thirty-three. Multi-millionaire by the time I was twenty-eight. Eighty per

cent owner of a large group of companies, some of
which are located overseas and one of which is a film
company, based in this country. This house stands in
two hundred acres of land, every boundary of which is
humming with security precautions, controlled from the
gatehouse we passed.'

He hadn't mentioned whether or not he was married,
Gina noticed.

'Why the security precautions?'

'Various reasons. Among other things, this place is a
treasure house of antiques.'

'And?'

'Excuse me,' he said abruptly, 'I must make the
telephone call I spoke of. If you've finished your tea,
ring the bell and Mrs Bush will show you round. I'll see
you at dinner.'

The tour of the main areas of the house left Gina
bewildered. Even then there was a whole wing and the
attics left unexplored.

'How can one man possibly live in all this?' she asked
the friendly housekeeper.

'Bless you, miss. It's never empty! Later on today it'll
be swarming with people. It always is when Mr Tod is
filming.'

'Filming? Here?'

'Bushie! Bushie! Is he home yet? *Is* he?'

A very diminutive person erupted from a room Gina
had not entered, a little doll of a girl, with saucer-wide
sapphire eyes and jet black hair that bubbled in natural
curls. This unexpected apparition was followed by an
apologetic young woman in a nursemaid's uniform.

'I'm so sorry, Mrs Bush. I did tell Miss Melanie she
should wait until Mr Fallon sent for her. But she's been
so excited . . .'

'Who are *you*?' The child was staring up at Gina. At
first the blue eyes had been hostile, but now this was
replaced by puzzlement. 'At first I thought it was *her*.

You're very like her, but I think you're prettier and I think I might like you. *She's* horrid!'

Gina wondered with some amusement which of the child's female acquaintances had warranted such rancour.

'That will do, Miss Melanie.' Mrs Bush spoke firmly, though her expression was indulgent. Gina guessed that the housekeeper sympathised with the child's feelings about the unknown. 'Miss Darcy doesn't want to be bothered with your nonsense just now.'

'Are you staying here?' The dark-haired mite was evidently aware of the housekeeper's partiality. 'Are you going to be in my daddy's films?'

Tod Fallon was this child's father? Gina knew just why her heart rose so sickeningly in her throat, preventing speech.

'*She's* in his films,' Melanie continued.

'Melanie,' the nursemaid intervened, 'you heard what Mrs Bush said. Now back to the nursery for your tea. Miss Darcy will want to unpack and rest.'

'All right.' The child responded to the urging hand, but over her shoulder she had a parting word for Gina. 'Will you play with me sometimes, when you're not tired?'

Protests from housekeeper and nursemaid that Gina's presence at Mallions was not principally for Melanie's entertainment fell on unheeding ears, and the child fixed Gina with a penetrating stare which demanded an answer.

'I'd like that, Melanie,' she said truthfully, 'so long as your daddy doesn't object. I'm here to work, you see.'

With this the child appeared satisfied and allowed herself to be led away, but the encounter had given Gina more food for thought than she relished. Tod Fallon had a daughter and therefore, presumably, a wife. She was dismayed by the strong disappointment this conclusion engendered.

Dinner, she realised Mrs Bush was warning her, would be a formal affair.

'Mr Tod always says it would be a crime to own a house like this and not live in it in the style to which it's accustomed.'

Gina was grateful for the housekeeper's hint. 'Will there be many other people at dinner?'

'Bless you, yes. It's rarely Mr Tod sits down with less than twenty.'

'He must have a lot of friends.'

'Technicians mostly,' Mrs Bush returned, 'actors and actresses. He's choosy who he calls friends.'

Left alone in the white-walled, low-beamed, chintzy bedroom, Gina considered what she should wear for her first dinner party at Mallions. Thank goodness she had brought a large and varied selection from her wardrobe, even though Tod's eyes had risen a visible inch or two at the number of suitcases he'd been required to fit into the boot of the Rolls Royce.

The house, which earlier had seemed so vast and silent, was beginning to come alive. Gina could hear the movement of feet over the groaning boards of stairs and passageways; the sound of water tormenting the joints of ancient plumbing; men's and women's voices raised in conversation and laughter.

The minx! Tod thought, as Gina paused deliberately in the doorway, her gaze coolly sweeping the room. Did she realise the effectiveness of her late arrival? Of course she did. She was a consummate, natural actress. That damned Jimmy Riley had been hiding her light for too long.

She looked magnificent, her red hair lending a rich glow to the magnolia skin of face, neck and shoulders. The silky black bodice of her simple dress covered one shoulder only, leaving the other dramatically bare; the long full skirt with its matching tie belt was white, with enormous black polka dots. Her outfit was simplicity itself.

'This is Gina, everyone. Gina, let me introduce you to some of the people you'll be working with.'

There followed a succession of names and faces which, she was sure, would take her months to assimilate. She could not doubt the genuine warmth of her greeting from the men, but Gina, often intuitive, recognised the barely polite aloofness of the majority of the women.

At the table, she was seated between the two singularly large and muscular men, Greg and Andy. Stuntmen, she hazarded? The younger of the two, about her own age, was open in his admiration of her.

'Greg Gibson,' he introduced himself. 'We'd no idea old Tod was bringing along such a stunning addition to our number. He has a pretty taste in redheads.' Over a lull in the conversation, his voice carried quite clearly and Gina was aware of Tod's sudden frowning gaze upon them. 'Of course, it's obvious why he picked *you*,' Greg was continuing, when Tod interrupted him, his voice unusually harsh, even for Tod.

'I haven't explained our project to Gina yet and I'd prefer to do so myself.' It wasn't a request but a definite command, issued, not just to Greg, but generally. Gina sensed the surprise of those around her.

'Sure thing, Tod. You're the boss!' Greg said, but the puzzled look remained on his ruggedly handsome features for some time as he turned the conversation into other channels.

This interchange increased Gina's unease. She'd had the idea all along that there was some underlying motive for Tod's selection of her for special training. She had never really been able to believe in his dedication to improving *Fantasy Woman*. As he'd said on the occasion of their first meeting, it just wasn't his kind of television.

As she might have expected in Tod's home, the meal was superb, five courses following each other in smooth, efficient succession, and she enjoyed the food, despite her awareness of covert glances from the other women around her. Not one of them was a redhead. What had Greg meant?

Only a girl seated directly opposite seemed disposed to be friendly. 'I'm Debbie. Never mind the second name. It's bad enough having to remember first names when you're plunged into a whole crowd of people.'

At the end of the meal, there was a general movement to leave the dining-room.

'Gina!' Without a word of apology, Tod interrupted her conversation with Debbie. 'I'd like to see you in the library, now.' He didn't wait for her agreement, but turned on his heel, striding away as though he confidently expected her to follow him. Like a dog called to heel! she thought indignantly.

Determined that she was going to set the pattern for their future relationship, she lingered deliberately, pursuing the topic she and Debbie had been discussing. But all the while, she noticed the younger girl throwing anxious glances towards the door.

'If ... if Tod wants you, hadn't you better go?' Debbie said at last. 'He ... he doesn't like to be kept waiting.'

'Is that so?' Gina said. 'Then perhaps it's time someone *made* him wait.'

A tall, statuesque blonde nearby overheard their exchange.

'Perhaps Gina has a special dispensation, Deborah darling. After all, it does rather look as if he's traded in the old model for a new one, doesn't it? His last redhead fawned on him disgustingly.'

Debbie flushed scarlet.

'Shut up, Stephanie!' she muttered. 'You heard what Tod said. You know we weren't to . . .'

'Gina!' Greg was at her elbow, apologetic, but determined. 'Tod sent me to get you.'

For a moment she contemplated prolonging her defiance, then decided that she'd made her point sufficiently clear.

'See you later,' she told Debbie, then accompanied Greg, her pace a deliberate stroll. He left her outside the library door.

Tod was seated behind the large desk, a script laid out in front of him. He was just in the act of banging down the telephone receiver and it was obvious that not all his irritation was caused by Gina's tardiness. Just as apparently, however, he intended to take it out on her.

'When I say I want to see you, I mean right away, not half an hour later!'

She was determined not to appear daunted by his manner, not to forsake the stand she had taken.

'If you'd asked me politely, I wouldn't have kept you waiting,' she said coolly, taking the chair his impatiently gesturing hand indicated, leaning back to indicate her complete ease. 'I'm accustomed to a certain amount of civility from my employers.'

'Then you'll have to get reaccustomed!' he snapped. 'Don't come the starlet with me. You may have been big time on TV, but here you're nobody until I make you somebody. I'm a busy man; I haven't time for pussy-footing around. When I say jump, that's just what people do.'

'Not me!' she retorted. Then, before he could make an angry answer, she leant forward in her chair, fixing him with a keen glance of her green eyes. 'You want my co-operation, Mr Fallon. For some reason you appear to want it very badly, or you wouldn't have gone to the lengths you have to secure it. If you're the kind of man you purport to be, you'd have given up on me long since, told me to get lost. I wonder why you didn't?' She leant back, crossing one shapely silk-clad leg over the other, aware that he was watching the movement, that he couldn't hide his interested reaction to it. 'You *need* my co-operation and you can have it, but on my terms; and you must admit they're not very onerous. Simple courtesy, the odd "please" and "thank you", won't cost you money.'

'You cool little bitch!' But there was a grudging admiration, rather than anger, in his tone. 'All right, thank you for deigning to answer my summons. And now,' his tone altered once again to impatient briskness, 'd'you mind if we get down to business?'

She knew it had been a sarcastic, rhetorical question, requiring no reply, but she answered, nevertheless.

'Not at all. In fact I'm dying to have the mystery solved. Why all the secrecy? Why weren't the others allowed to discuss it with me?'

'Briefly,' he told her, 'we're in the process of making a film, a fast-moving thriller, something on the lines of a James Bond except that the agent is a woman. But that doesn't mean there'll be any punches pulled. Anything a male agent can perform, this woman can equal.'

'Excepting in the sexual field, of course?' Gina asked, mock seriously. 'You won't be expecting her to pull birds?'

He missed her straight-faced humour.

'Use your head!' he snapped. 'Obviously it's the other way around. She's as ruthless in her use of men as Bond of his women. The whole point of this briefing is to warn you that the stunts aren't going to be easy. There'll be no faking, no trick photography. You'll be earning your salary, *if* you pass through your training successfully.'

'But what's any of this got to do with *Fantasy*

Woman?'

'Not a thing,' he startled her by admitting, but only confirming her earlier suspicions.

'But you said . . .'

'Good God, woman! Don't you realise you're being given an opportunity in a million, an opportunity to break away from that third-rate rubbish?'

'But why was it necessary to lie, to let me think . . . ?'

'Because you might have refused, out of some ridiculous sense of loyalty towards the programme, to Riley.'

'Jimmy doesn't know about this?'

'Of course!' Coldly, 'It was only fair to give him an opportunity to replace you.'

Gina leapt to her feet.

'You high-handed bastard! You might at least have given me the choice!'

'And what would that choice have been?'

Trapped, she stumbled over her reply.

'I . . . I . . .'

'You'd have chosen to move on. *You* know it; *I* know it. So don't let's have any hypocritical claptrap.'

The fact that the adjective was apt did nothing to improve Gina's mood, but she let it pass. His words so far had conjured up bright attractive images that she wanted to hear confirmed. If she were to train for all the skills necessary to Tod's dauntless heroine, this, by implication, must mean that she was to play the role. Surely stardom didn't come that easily? Her day-dreaming was interrupted.

'Don't you want to know any more about your duties?'

Duties? A strange way of putting it, but then this was an unfamiliar world.

'Yes, of course I do.'

'Right. I understand you swim and ride passably well. Anything else?'

He *was* well-informed.

'I've recently taken up judo.'

'Done any running?'

'At school, hundred-yard sprints, that sort of thing,' but he was shaking his head impatiently.

'This will call for stamina. Cross-country would have been more useful. Right.' He made a note on a pad in front of him. 'We'll put daily jogging on your schedule.'

Obviously, Gina though wryly, this job was to be no sinecure; but then she hadn't expected that it would be.

'You asked about swimming and riding?' she queried. 'Will they be of use?'

'Well. You'll be expected to scuba dive; to learn how to make a horse fall; how to fall from a horse yourself, without breaking your neck.'

'You must have a large staff of tutors.'

'Not at all,' he contradicted. 'Most of your training I'll undertake personally.'

'But ...' Gina couldn't hide the discomposure this intelligence caused her and he smiled his amusement.

'I wasn't born a director, you know. I started out as a stuntman and found that a stuntman must also be an actor. In fact I still act in my own films and I still perform my own stunts.'

'Are ... are you acting in *this* particular film?'

'Naturally!'

'As ... as what?'

'Since you're so interested, not that it will affect *you* much, as the man who finally outruns, outrides and generally tames the wild cat of a heroine.'

Why wouldn't it affect her? She'd have to act opposite him!

'I met your daughter before dinner!' Gina blurted out the words.

Tod's dark eyebrows rose.

'Oh? I fail to see what that has to do with our present discussion.'

'N-nothing really. I just remembered it. She ... she asked if I would play with her sometimes. I said I'd find out if that was all right with you.'

His face still bore a look of incredulity.

'You're not here as a nursemaid for my daughter. The one she has is perfectly adequate. Besides which,' his expression became sardonic, 'you'll have little time, or energy, left for playing games, of any kind.'

'And just what does that imply?' she asked, though his tone had carried an unmistakable hint of his meaning.

'That I don't encourage liaisons between members of my team while a film is in process. It distracts them, prevents them giving of their best. Stay away from the men, Gina! I've already noted your dramatic effect on Greg.'

'Have you?' she retorted. 'I accept that I'm here to work for you; and if you refuse to let me make friends with your daughter, I'll accept that, too, though I think it's a shame. She seems to lead a lonely life, shut up in the nursery, only seeing you when you condescend to summon her, as you do your employees. But I won't accept your right to dictate my other friendships.'

Tod's face darkened to a frightening intensity and, as he pushed back his chair and rose from behind the desk, Gina took a backward step towards the door.

'My daughter, though it's none of your business, leads a secluded life for a very good reason, a reason which also gives me the right to decide whose company she seeks. It's true I can't physically prevent you from making assignations with Greg, or with any other man here; but if anyone's work suffers, you'll be the one out on your ear. You may think you have me in a cleft stick, because I so obviously needed a redhead, but you're not unique. If I have to, I can afford to search the length and breadth of the world to find a replacement.'

'Then why didn't you?' she taunted. 'Why pick on me?'

'Oh, don't get any big ideas about your own talent; you haven't any until I drum it into you. You were simply available!'

Available? What exactly did he mean by that? She couldn't voice her suspicions, but she could put the record straight, subtly.

'You needn't worry!' She injected scorn into her voice. 'I'm not interested in Greg or any of the men here, you included. I came here to work. You'll get your money's worth!'

'Oh, I will!' he said with dauntingly grim assurance. Then, coming to tower over her, the closed door barring her escape, 'As for your other point, your total lack of interest in men, don't try to fool yourself, Gina! You forget,' he said softly, 'I've held you in my arms. I know just how little it takes to bring that body of yours flooding back to life. You may have had it in deep freeze for the last year or so, but it wouldn't take much to start a thaw. I've done it once. I can do it again.'

She gasped at his presumption, sought for words to deflate his pretensions, to cool the dark warmth she could see deepening in his eyes.

'Sorry to disappoint you,' she gibed, 'but instant coffee, instant snacks I've learnt to put up with; instant sex doesn't turn me on at all.'

It had been a mistake to provoke him, to issue what he must only see as a challenge. She realised that at once from the expression on his face. And simultaneously with her recognition of his intention his arm shot out, snaking around her waist, hauling her, tall as she was, clear of the floor and hard up against him. At once her violent trembling betrayed her own rising desire, which not even his triumphant words could quell.

'No? I think I've just disproved that.'

CHAPTER FIVE

His hand reached behind her for the key of the library door, turning it, securing the room against intrusion or escape.

'I warn you,' she said breathlessly against the bronzed flesh of his throat, 'I shall scream.'

He lowered his head, his breath fanning her temple, his mouth nuzzling the point of her cheekbone.

'Scream away! No one's going to come to your assistance.'

She tried to keep her tone light, sarcastic, tried to lean away from him.

'They'll think you're giving me my first acting lesson, I suppose?'

'Possibly,' he agreed drily. 'In any event,' he mumbled the words down the side of her neck, 'no one would dare to intrude.'

Frantically, Gina's fists pushed against his shoulders.

'Oh? Not even your wife? Isn't *she* curious about what you get up to with actresses, behind locked doors?'

'I should hardly thinks so, no, since she's been dead for some years.'

'Oh!' Gina gasped, shock almost deadening all other reactions to this intelligence. He was free then? But she didn't know whether or not she should express conventional sorrow. How could he speak so callously, so unfeelingly? Didn't he have any heart, any regrets for the mother of that lovely little girl upstairs? But she was given no opportunity to voice her opinion, to ask her question.

'Shall we get on with the experiment?' he asked

huskily. It wasn't a question, but a declaration of intent.

She began to struggle more violently, but he had her backed hard against the door.

'Let me go! Don't you dare!'

'Oh, but I *do* dare.' One arm was completely encircling her, holding her immobile, his free hand performing the same service for her chin, so that she was powerless to evade the dark, descending head, the threat of the firm, shapely mouth lowered to hers.

She gave a little moan in her throat as her lips parted to his ruthless invasion of them. Her head forced back against the hard panels of the door, kept there by the pressure of his mouth, left his hand free to go marauding over her body, caressing the shoulder bared by the sophisticated drape of her dress, revealing the other shoulder to match, then sliding the silky material to her waist, seeking the softness of her breasts, necessarily, because of the cut of the dress, un-encumbered by a bra.

Hard, exploratory fingers brushed vulnerable peaks, played provocatively with them, until of themselves they seemed to strain against his hand, inviting further, tantalising caresses. She knew she was letting him prove his outrageous claim, but somehow there was nothing she could do about it; she didn't want him to stop, ever.

His mouth moved on now, descending to her breasts, then lower still, growing impatient of the remaining barrier caused by the folds of her dress. He fumbled for the zip, dealt competently with it, and Gina felt the material cascade down over hips and thighs to pool about her feet. Now only the scantiest triangle of lace protected her and as his hand sought to explore beneath it, she went curiously still, even the trembling of her body ceased, as, with a cold shock, sanity returned.

'All right, damn you! You've proved your point! But

that's as far as you go. Now let me get the hell out of here.'

He met her damp-eyed defiance with an implacable stare.

'Conceding victory so soon? And it was just getting interesting!'

But he released her and watched with what appeared to be clinical detachment as she bent to retrieve her dress with hands whose trembling she could not conceal, though she hoped he was not aware that her whole body vibrated with an unassuaged quivering; he seemed so cool, so unperturbed.

In reality, Tod was finding great difficulty holding himself in check. He had been on the point, he knew, of removing that final garment, of carrying her to one of the chesterfields, of taking his seduction scene to its ultimate conclusion. But something had prevented him. A belated sense of loyalty to the absent Marcha? Strangely, he didn't think so. True, there had been no other women in his life since he'd met Marcha. Physically she was all that a man could desire, always avid for his possession of her, a demanding, skilful lover. They were well matched, he and Marcha, but without any emotional complications, and that was all he wanted, wasn't it: the satisfaction of his natural needs?

Something else, something to which he couldn't put a name, had stopped him making love to Gina, and it hadn't been her belated show of resistance. That, he could have overcome, but suddenly he hadn't wanted to see her like this—an unwilling victim!

He unlocked the library door, holding it wide open for her.

'That will be all for the moment,' he said formally, for the benefit of anyone within earshot. 'It would be as well if you went to bed now. You've a long day ahead of you.'

'Sunday?' she said, protest in her voice, despite her

still uncontrollable shaking.

'In this house, Sunday is like any other day. Breakfast is served from seven-thirty. At eight-thirty you'll be out on the airstrip, suitably dressed for climbing in and out of an aircraft. Sleep well!'

He couldn't know what a mockery those last words were. How would she manage to sleep at all now? She'd known they would come some time, the flying lessons, but at least she'd believed herself to have one more day's grace in which to steel herself. She sidled past him, careful to avoid the slightest contact between their bodies, and made for the stairs.

But, honest with herself, she knew that it wasn't just the thought of tomorrow's lessons that kept her awake until the small hours, and, when she did sleep, her dreams were troubled and erotic.

Gina was glad to discover, next morning, that Tod had already breakfasted. At least he wasn't there to note and comment upon her lack of appetite, speculate as to its cause. As it was, the one piece of toast, which was all she dared eat, clung to the roof of her mouth with the consistency of blotting paper. Hastily, she washed it down with hot, strong coffee.

Inexorably, the hands of the clock crept nearer to eight-thirty and at last she could procrastinate no longer. The idly drifting windsock pointed out her direction and she was standing beside the aircraft hangar with exactly a minute to spare as Tod taxied out on to the runway.

She had been uncertain what to wear, settling finally for an emerald green track suit and tying back her tumbling red hair with a matching, silky ribbon.

Without any preliminaries, Tod ordered her into the plane, which looked extremely small and frail to Gina's nervous eyes. He told her to pay attention while he demonstrated first the bewildering array of controls and then innumerable take-offs and landings.

All the while, Gina remained rigid with fright. For her the next hour passed in a haze, her brain scarcely functioning as she struggled to give intelligent answers to his remarks, to take in what he was saying.

This procedure was repeated twice daily for a week and she received no kid-glove treatment from Tod. This was no hobby to be practised in idle moments, he emphasised. You persevered and if you couldn't take it, there was no point in continuing. Nor could you bluff your way through it.

'You can't fake an aptitude for flying. Either you can do it or, if you can't, you stick at it for hour after hour until you can.'

Once or twice during that week, to her horror, he demonstrated looping the loop.

'Not that you'll ever be called upon to perform one yourself, but it's as well to know the technique in case of accident, to know how to get out of one. Watch! You apply full opposite rudder, at the same time pushing the stick into forward position.'

However, by the end of the week, she was surprised to find that her mind was beginning to take in what it was all about, that she was beginning to conquer her fears. There came a morning when she was able to eat a hearty breakfast and set out for the airstrip full of enthusiasm and an intense curiosity to discover her own limitations, for that day she was to take the controls herself, with Tod at her side.

One thing lacking during the past few days, she realised with gratitude, had been any sense of embarrassment in his company. She'd been concentrating far too hard on conquering her fears to have time for indulging other emotions. And even though she felt more at ease in the little aircraft, there were new problems to contend with. Now the martinet at her side was informing her that, despite his presence, she was totally responsible for their safety.

It was hard physical work, too, she found, wrestling with a heavy plane; for, despite its deceptively fragile appearance, the Cessna was no featherweight to control by fingertip touch.

It was during the second week that she realised she was no longer afraid of actually being in the plane, that she was even enjoying herself, just so long as Tod was there to take care of any emergencies. But this euphoria was short-lived, for it dawned on her that the more she improved, the sooner he would make her go up alone. This thought actually impaired her progress for a couple of days, her blunders earning her bellows and harsh words from her inflexible instructor, bringing her almost, but not quite, to the verge of tears. She would *not* give way to such weakness before him! And his tactics worked where kindly patience might not have done, making Gina stubbornly determined to prove herself.

Then, one morning, after a series of practice take-offs and landings, Tod announced that he was getting out.

'Tod!' Panic-stricken she called after his departing figure. 'Please! Not yet! I'm not ready!'

He ignored her pleas and turned to gesture impatiently, indicating that she should take off.

Hands shaking, her lips muttering imprecations against the tyrant, she went through the motions. She had never been so scared in all her life. This was worse than her one flight in a commercial aircraft. How could she have been scared by that? At least then she had been in the competent hands of a qualified, experienced pilot. Now she was mistress of her own fate.

Unaware that she was doing so, she recited the take-off ritual aloud, only assimilating, some considerable time later, the fact that she was actually flying; the altimeter told her that she was at nine hundred feet above the ground; the realisation had a strange, heady effect upon her.

She'd done it! She was supposed to land now, but her new confidence, the exaltation she felt, made that seem too tame a proceeding. Far off to her right, her attention was caught by the sight of another plane. Its yellow body small against the vastness of the sky, it cavorted around, practising aerobatics. The pricklings of a crazy desire invaded her being, a desire as strong, as compulsive as that of sexual stimulation. Could she? *Dared* she?

Without giving herself time to think, she turned Tod's Cessna into a rather ragged barrel roll. What had he said? 'Opposite rudder, stick forward'? It worked like a dream! She repeated the performance again and again, until suddenly the loop was a perfect, graceful arc, the machine she flew an extension of her being in a satisfying oneness, like the coming together of man and woman.

Now she was content to come down to earth, making a perfect three-point landing, taxiing to within a few feet of where Tod stood, by the hangar.

She released her harness, sprang from the plane, ran towards him, her lovely features alight with jubilation.

'I did it! I did it! *I can fly!* Did you see me?'

'I saw you all right, you bloody little fool!' His face was grey, drawn into grim lines, as he grabbed her arm and dragged her into the hangar. 'What the hell did you think you were doing up there? You were supposed to take off, do a few bumps and circuits and then land, not behave like a bloody flying circus. You haven't had enough experience for that sort of thing. Suppose you'd crashed the plane?'

His anger, its violent expression, quelled her exuberance, and anti-climax took over as she realised he was right. In her excitement at her own achievement, her triumph over fear, she had become over-confident, foolhardly even. Her legs began to shake with reaction and tears trembled on her eyelashes as with a quivering voice she sought to take out her sudden sense of mortification on him.

'*If* I'd crashed, I suppose I'd have been killed and your precious aeroplane would have been a write-off. But that wouldn't have mattered so much, would it? You're rich! You could go out and buy another plane, like some people buy a bicycle. And as you said yourself, redheads are two a penny.'

But not this one, Tod thought savagely, as her legs finally gave under her and she would have fallen, if his arms had not gone around her in a steely hold. Unable to think, to feel beyond this moment, he lowered himself on to a pile of crumpled tarpaulins, taking her with him, kissing the salty tears from her eyelids, planting fierce little kisses all over her damp, pale cheeks.

'Don't ever do anything like that to me again!' he groaned, before his mouth took hers, hungrily, mercilessly.

She turned her head from side to side, trying to evade him, but to no purpose. His kiss was blistering her lips, his hands were seeking the lower edge of her track suit top, lifting it up so that he could curve his fingers about her breasts, exploring her body as though he would reassure himself that she had come to no physical harm.

Did he *care* that she had put herself into danger? She felt her body's involuntary surge against his, recognised their mutual arousal for what it was, an urgent, primitive response to the danger in which she had placed herself, a heady, frightening excitement, more powerful than any aphrodisiac.

He ripped the top off, over her head, burying his face between her breasts, his hands warm and proprietary upon her, hands that were beginning to move lower, gradually easing down the track suit trousers, stroking her stomach, shaping her hips.

With a little moan of pleasure she wound her arms

around his neck, holding his head tightly to her breasts, loving the feel of his crisp hair against her skin.

'Let's get rid of these damned trousers,' he murmured thickly, and she didn't argue. Scorching desire rode her; the last of the icy barrier she had constructed around her had melted away.

His body was crushing her and, greatly daring, she felt for the waistband of his trousers. The ache in the pit of her stomach was becoming intolerable.

'Tod! Oh, Tod!' she whispered. 'Help me! Please help me!' Frustratingly, her trembling fingers could not master the task she had set them.

But suddenly, all in one fluid movement, he rolled over, thrusting her away from him. Rising to his feet, he strode to the door of the hangar and stood there, staring out over the airstrip. In the sudden silence, Gina could hear the drone of the little yellow aircraft, still performing its aerobatics, and it seemed to her that this moment would be forever imprinted on her memory with that accompanying sound.

'Tod?' Her voice was barely above a whisper. 'Tod? What is it? What's wrong?'

He did not answer for a moment or two, but flexed his shoulders, as if they bore an intolerable burden, ran his hand through his hair, trying to restore some order to the devastation her fingers had created. Then he turned towards her, his voice harsh, barely under control.

'*I'm* wrong! That's what it is!'

'But why? Don't you ... don't you want me?' Still her voice was barely audible, but he heard her.

'Damn you, Gina!' His voice shook with anger. 'Of course I wanted you. I still do, confound it!'

'Then ... then why?' she repeated. She didn't care that all the defences she'd ever erected had come crashing down. For a few moments, she had been alive again, gloriously alive. She had wanted Tod and he had wanted her. Where was the problem? She couldn't believe that he hadn't made love to dozens of women, before and since his marriage.

'Because ... because ... Oh, to hell with it, just because! For God's sake, Gina, take that look off your face. Get up and get dressed. Go back to the house. If it's any consolation, you've passed your flying test with honours.'

'But I didn't pass *yours*? Is that it?' The tears began to pour down her cheeks and she made to run past him. But the sight of her tear-stained face and hurt eyes was too much for him and he barred her way, holding her, crushing her against him, his body still hard against hers in arousal.

'Gina, Gina, for God's sake, don't cry,' he groaned. 'I can't stand it. I'm only human!'

'You're not,' she gulped. 'You're ... you're inhuman, to be able to stop, just like that, to be so cruel . . .'

'Damn it! Haven't you ever heard of being cruel to be kind? What would have happened, if I'd made love to you? Would that have been the last of it? You know it wouldn't. Women are all the same, with only a few exceptions. You'd have wanted some commitment from me and I can't give it.' But he buried his face in her neck and his body shook.

'I see!' In control of herself again now, desire effectively dampened by his words, she pulled free of him. 'Thank you for the flying instruction and,' bitterly, 'the *other* lesson. You're a good teacher in the school of hard knocks.'

She turned on her heel and marched away, head held high, shoulders back. Tod Fallon would never see her cry again. What a fool she had been to lower her guard, to let herself believe that there was something special about this man.

Half-way across the field, she halted, struck by a sudden thought. Surely it couldn't be anything to do with that ridiculous rule of his, no fraternising between the sexes during filming? Did he adhere to his own rules? No. She couldn't believe that. There had to be some stronger, more valid reason for his rejection of her. Another woman? That was more likely. She continued on her way.

Tod had watched her retreat, unbearably touching in its determined dignity. He had seen her pause. He held his breath. Did she mean to turn around, come back, make one last appeal? Almost he found himself hoping that she would. Knew that if she did, this time he would be unable to leash his desires, that he would have to make her his. But her pause was short-lived. She marched on as doggedly as ever, and he heard himself utter a single sigh, a mixture of disappointment and relief.

By the time he, too, returned to the house, he was fully in command of himself once more. Gina must continue her training; she must be ready by his deadline to commence filming. He wished now that he *could* hand her over to some other tutor, but, not given to false modesty, he knew he was the best tutor she could have.

He was not the only one to wish that her further training was in other hands. After dinner that evening, a cool, composed Gina sought him out in the library, standing poised in the open doorway, ready for instant departure should the need arise.

'Come in!' he growled. 'Shut the door! I don't bite!' Then his skin colour deepened beneath his tan at the unfortunate choice of words; for he *had* bitten her that morning, nibbling enticingly at her breasts, and they both remembered it.

'No thanks!' Her own face flushed, she remained where she was. 'I can say what I have to say from here.

I want a different trainer. I want you to let Greg or one of the others teach me my job.'

He gave a short laugh.

'If any of them were capable, I'd grant your request, believe me! But Greg's no stuntman. Nor are any of the others.'

'But . . . but he looks like . . .'

'Greg and Andy are here as bodyguards. You may not have noticed, but one or the other of them is always around. They're never off duty together.'

'Bodyguards? Who needs them? Not you surely?' she mocked disbelievingly.

'Not me,' he agreed. 'I can take care of myself. They're here to protect Melanie.'

'Your daughter? Why should *she* need protection, and from whom?'

His face was drawn into stern lines and she realised she was trespassing.

'That's a long story, an old, unhappy one; I've no wish to resurrect it. Besides, it doesn't concern you.'

'All right!' She turned on her heel. 'I get the message. Mind my own business. That will be easy. I'm not remotely interested in anything that concerns you.' It should have been a good exit, but,

'Gina!' His abrupt use of her name halted her in midstride. 'Wear riding clothes tomorrow.'

She swung around. Tomorrow! They'd only just completed a gruelling flying course. Was there to be no break, no relaxation? He caught her thoughts from her expression.

'We're working to a tight schedule. In another fortnight, we start the actual filming. If you thought learning to fly was tough, think again! The riding will take us all of that fortnight, maybe more. It depends on you. Think you can take it?'

'I can take it,' she told him confidently.

'You're not scared of horses I suppose?'

'Of course not!' Her eyes widened in surprise. 'Why should I be?'

'You were terrified of the Cessna at first,' he said bluntly.

'I . . .' Her words of denial trailed away at the certainty in his face. 'How did you . . . ?'

'But you've got guts, Gina.' His tone was suddenly gentle, disarming, his voiced admiration genuine, she could swear. He took a step towards her. 'You were petrified, yet you never said a word. You went through with it, conquered your fear. How?'

She had retreated before his advance and despite his changed mood, or perhaps because of it, she was even more on the defensive.

'How?' Nervous tension lent a sharp edge to her voice. 'You need to ask me that, after all the cracks you made at me the very first time we met? I've a long memory. I swore I'd never give you a chance to call me a coward, ever again.'

'No,' he agreed, much to her amazement. 'I was wrong. You're not a coward, Gina, not in that way. It takes great courage to face and overcome physical fear.'

She was in physical fear now, but it stemmed from his increasing proximity. He had ably demonstrated his power to arouse her, yet each time he had demonstrated that he was only playing with her, that the undoubted chemistry between them meant nothing to him. She stepped backwards into the hallway.

'Good night!' she said, coldly formal. 'Will half-past-eight be suitable for the riding instruction?'

'Greg?' Gina came downstairs just as the security man was leaving the breakfast room. 'Can you spare me a moment?'

'Any number of them!' He grinned and followed her as she made a selection from the heavily laden sideboard. 'In fact I could spare you a few hours, if you'd only say the word. It's my evening off. How about it?'

Gina hesitated. Despite her defiant words to Tod about her right to choose her own friends, she didn't really want to go out with Greg.

'All right,' she said hesitantly and then, aware that it was hardly a gracious acceptance, 'thank you. I'd like that,' and she allowed her face to relax into the dazzling smile that had floored many men before Greg Gibson.

Tod, putting his head into the breakfast room to see if she was there, witnessed the smile. Grim-faced, he told her that he was ready when she was and withdrew. Oh dear. Obviously Tod thought she'd been chatting Greg up.

'That's great!' Greg said, his own grin widening. 'Say!' he halted in the doorway, 'you were going to ask me something?'

'Oh! Oh yes, but it wasn't that important. It can wait till tonight now, when we've more time. I daren't be late for my riding lesson.' She smiled wryly, jerking her head in the direction Tod had taken.

'Oh yeah!' His tone was disbelieving. 'You're the first woman we've had here who didn't jump whenever Tod cracked the whip. But by all means leave it till tonight. See you!' His complacent expression as he departed told Gina that he believed she'd waylaid him for a purpose, that all she'd been after was a date with him.

She gritted her teeth. Maybe she'd been too hasty in her agreement.

'You mean we're actually going outside the "Berlin Wall"?'

The Rolls Royce had swept around the perimeter of the house and crunched down the long gravelled drive towards the massive gates.

'We need the facilities of an indoor arena!' Tod's manner was brusque and Gina prepared to lapse into silence for the remainder of the journey. But to her surprise, he continued to speak, still in the same abrupt manner, and she sensed his reluctance even while he imparted the information. 'I suppose I can't blame you for your curiosity. It must seem a strange set-up we have here.'

'It is rather like a prisoner-of-war camp,' she returned lightly, as the gates clanged to behind them, 'but I've no desire to pry, provided *I'm* not a prisoner here. I *should* like a day off sometime!'

'You're free to come and go as you wish. As I told you last night, these precautions are for Melanie's sake. As to days off, we'll see!'

'I suppose,' Gina said slowly, feeling her way, 'that there are bound to be risks involved in being a rich man's child, being kidnapped, held to ransom?'

'Yes,' he acknowledged. 'It is kidnapping I fear; not for the sake of money, though, but of vendetta.'

'"Vendetta".' She repeated the word incredulously. 'It sounds like something out of an Italian gangster movie, the Mafia, family feuds.'

'Maria, my wife, was Italian. I met her when I was making a circus documentary in La Spezia, Italy. She was a trapeze artiste, part of a family act, the "Flying Mantalinis". To cut the story short,' there was pain in Tod's voice as if the telling hurt still, 'I saw a lot of Maria. We fell in love, Her family weren't pleased, because it broke up the act. But we married, came back to this country and, a year later, Melanie was born.'

'Did ... did Maria die in childbirth?' Gina asked gently.

'It might have been better if she had. At least that would have been one of life's natural hazards, an act of God. Then the Mantalinis might not have blamed me for her death.' They were travelling faster now, almost as if Tod sought to escape from the horrors of the past. 'Maria had been brought up to circus life. Danger was

the breath of life to her. Without her family, she could
no longer do trapeze work, so she pestered me to let her
become one of my stuntwomen.'

'And did you let her?'

'Not at first. I wanted to keep her apart from my
work. I wanted her to be my wife, Melanie's mother, to
grace my home.'

His words held bitter memories for Gina, too,
carrying as they did a recollection of Keith's feelings on
the same subject.

'But performing was in her blood. She needed
excitement, challenge. Finally I let her have her way,
and lived to regret it. She was killed,' he concluded
bluntly, 'performing aerobatics, as you might have been
yesterday!'

Oh no! No wonder he had been so furious, so shaken.
During her thoughtless stunting, he had been reliving
his wife's death, expecting to see a re-enactment of the
tragedy that had killed her. In his anger, in his relief,
had it been Maria that he had taken in his arms? Had
he wanted to make believe, just for a few moments, that
it was his wife who had survived?

'But where do the Mantalinis come into this? Why
the vendetta?'

'They blamed me, of course,' he said impatiently, 'for
allowing Maria to fly.'

'But it was her idea!'

'In Italy,' Tod's tone was heavy, 'the women obey
their fathers, their brothers and finally their husbands.
Old Mantalini contends that I was no fit husband for
his daughter and therefore no fit father for his
granddaughter.'

'I think that's most unfair,' Gina said hotly. 'He let
Maria risk her life on the trapeze.'

Tod shook his dark head sadly.

'There was little danger for Maria. Oh, some, I grant
you. But surrounded by her father and six brothers,

who wouldn't have seen one hair of her head harmed . . .? But I, her husband, let her go up, alone, in an aeroplane. There's no safety net to catch you when you fall from the sky.'

'And Melanie? The bodyguards?' Horror widened Gina's beautiful eyes. 'Surely Mantalini wouldn't . . .? Oh he couldn't? Not a child?'

'He doesn't plan to kill her. She's his grandchild, after all. No, he wants her with him. Twice he's very nearly succeeded in snatching her, hence the precautions.'

'And what about you?' Gina's voice rose a nervous octave. 'Would . . . would he try to kill *you*?' How could Tod continue to move about the world as he did, knowing that at any moment he might be struck down by an assassin's knife, or by gunshot? It was in that moment of fear for him that Gina knew she loved Tod Fallon, and the shock of realisation was so great that it was only dimly she heard him say,

'No. Mantalini's no killer. His thugs only carry weapons to frighten. But he does want his revenge, and it would seem a fitting one to him to take away my daughter, as I deprived him of his.'

'But you can't keep Melanie locked up forever!' Gina protested, as Tod braked, skilfully easing the large car into a narrow turning. 'What sort of life would that be for a little girl? And what about when she grows up?'

'Mantalini can't live for ever. He's an old man now, and I hope, when he goes, his sons will drop the vendetta. I don't think they have the same heart for it.'

The road had brought them to some riding stables, a long, pristinely white house, flanked by outbuildings and a larger building which Tod told Gina was the indoor arena. 'Theresa had it built so she can give riding lessons all year round.'

As they got out of the car, Gina reflected ruefully that she need not have accepted Greg's offer of a date since, unexpectedly, Tod had provided her with all the answers to her questions. Still, she couldn't back out now. But she must make it clear to Greg that it was only a friendly, social occasion, that she wanted no complications, no involvements.

Because of that moment in the car, a moment of mingled fear and revelation, she found herself looking at Tod with new eyes as he strode across the stableyard towards the owner's office. She could have described him in detail with her eyes closed, so familiar had that splendid physique become, topped by the dark hair with its distinguished scattering of grey. Even though his back was towards her, his features were indelibly printed on her inner eye, the heavy brows spanning dark eyes, the forthright nose and assertive chin; and this, she marvelled, was the man with whom she had fallen in love.

'Gina! Get a move on!' His impatient voice recalled her wandering wits to the present and to the lowering remembrance that *he* was not interested in her, other than as a commodity. The morning's discoveries had explained a lot. She had been right in fancying that another woman lay between her and Tod; but the woman was his dead wife. Tod was still in love with Maria.

Theresa, who owned the stables, was a petite, energetic blonde. Her admiration for Tod was patently obvious, his manner towards her companionably affectionate, and Gina felt a stab of envy. How long had he known Theresa? The blonde girl had an advantage that Gina did not. She lived not too far away from Tod's home and it was obvious that their business arrangement brought them together quite often. Gina sighed. She had hoped that never again would she experience the jealousy syndrome. Now she knew she would resent any woman who came within Tod's orbit.

Twenty minutes later, elbows, knees, shoulders and hips heavily padded, she had something else to occupy her mind; she was finding out just what Tod had meant when he'd said that flying an aeroplane was nothing when it came to the risks and discomforts of horse stunting.

Over and over again she must practise falling to the sawdust of the indoor arena, learning just how to part company with the horse and turn in the air to get into the correct position. The aim was to fall backwards and sideways so that the first impact with the ground was with forearm and heel; thus she would finish in a face down position.

'You won't just be falling off willy-nilly, anywhere you like,' Tod explained, during a rest break. 'You'll be given a set spot and moment in which to do it. So you'll need to know the disposition of every camera, how much of the frame you and the horse are filling, the whereabouts of other actors and props.'

By the end of that morning's session, despite the heavy padding, Gina felt that every bone in her body was jarred, that every inch of flesh was bruised.

'Still want to be a stunt girl?' Tod asked, as Gina eased herself gingerly into his car.

She leant back against the silver grey upholstery, her answer, though positive, coming out on a weary sigh.

'Yes!'

'You see now why it requires a high standard of general fitness?'

'You can say that again!' It was a sardonic riposte, but Tod chose to take it seriously.

'I *do* say it again, *and* again. It's a subject in which your only tools are experience and more experience. The knowhow can only be handed down from a trained stuntman to the novice, either by word of mouth, or by demonstration.'

And Tod had used both methods, Gina thought,

almost asleep with fatigue. He'd bellowed instructions at her from the side of the ring, making her repeat the actions over and over again, until she was bone weary and almost on the point of rebellion. But he had also proved that he was capable of practising what he preached. Several times he had taken over her patient mount and shown her, by example, what he wanted. Yet he seemed totally untroubled by the numerous aches and pains that beset her. He must be fantastically fit.

As the iron gates closed them in once more, Tod glanced at her, noting her drawn face and closed eyes.

'Straight into a hot bath, the moment you get in,' he advised. 'This afternoon, we'll have a session in the swimming-pool.'

As she climbed the stairs to her room, Gina emitted the groans she had not allowed to escape her in front of Tod. The man was superhuman, or inhuman as she'd told him yesterday. Did he honestly expect her to have the strength to go on working on top of this morning's gruelling session?

The bath however did a lot to alleviate her discomfort and she was in a reasonably philosophical mood as she went down to lunch. Maybe swimming wouldn't be such a bad idea after all. It might complete the loosening up process.

Like breakfast, lunch in Tod's home was an informal, staggered meal, everyone eating of the cold collation as and when they had the time or the inclination, so that Gina was not surprised to find the dining-room empty, except for one person.

Standing with her back to the room, looking out of the window, the tall girl looked familiar, with her long fall of red hair and her statuesque height, and when, at the sound of Gina's heels in the parquet floor, the other swung around, Gina gave a gasp of recognition. But the surprise was mutual.

'What the hell are you doing here, Gina?' Then, with
shrill fury, 'The fool! The bloody fool! I told him not to
... But he just had to be right, as usual ... And of
course you wouldn't take much talking into it. *You*
wouldn't be able to resist...'

Now Gina was able to speak, voicing her own
shocked, bewildered surprise.

'Marcha! Why are *you* here?'

CHAPTER SIX

AFTER the break-up of Gina's marriage she'd thrown herself even more into her agency work, and through the agency had renewed her acquaintance with a distant cousin, whom she hadn't seen since childhood.

At that time, Marcha Durrant was a relative newcomer to the world of television, and a new programme had been conceived for her, a programme that would aim at gratifying people's private fantasies. Her producer had heard of the GD Agency and had suggested that she contact Gina, as the expert, for some ideas and advice.

'But I never dreamt it would be you!'

Marcha had wanted to talk about herself and her ambitions. It seemed that, as a relation, however distant, she expected Gina to help further her career. It was only some time later that Gina had been able to touch on her own life, to mention her marriage, its outcome, and that she had reverted to her maiden name. Even then Marcha's interest had been cursory, falsely sympathetic. Her manner implied that she, Marcha, would never have allowed her personal relationships to get into such a mess, nor would any man ever be permitted to thwart her will.

So, in the beginning, it had not been Gina who had worn the mask of Fantasy Woman, but Marcha. Despite the older girl's assiduous cultivation of her, Gina had not been deceived; she knew her cousin was working only towards her own ends and, as in childhood, she was unable to like or trust Marcha. Filled with a sense of her own importance at having a show of her own, Marcha displayed an unsympathetic,

almost brusque manner towards her guests, especially
when they failed abysmally at things they professed
themselves eager to do; and while Gina, in the
background, genuinely worried over the safety of
others, Marcha had no reservations about the quite
dangerous stunts ordinary people had, at first, been
allowed to attempt.

'If the fools want to break their silly necks, why
should I care?' was her standard retort, when, at
planning meetings, Gina had essayed a protest. Gina
had been right to fear that some day there would be a
dreadful accident, but it was no consolation to her that
the format of the show was moderated only after such
an event had taken place.

When Marcha suddenly decided to abandon her
television career for one in films, Gina had been
startled, though flattered, when Jimmy Riley had
offered her the vacant role.

'I've no experience of working in television.' Despite
the irresistible temptation of a new challenge, she had
felt impelled to be honest.

'All the better,' the producer had retorted, 'we can
train *you* the way we want you to go. Besides, you've
been adviser to the series for the past six months; you
have some idea of what goes on; and you and Marcha
are physically so alike that, with that mask on, no one
will ever know there's been a change over.'

So, once more, she had put her advisory service into
the capable hands of her deputy and, not without some
trepidation, had assumed her new role. Despite the
fatigue she often felt, she enjoyed the travelling to
various locations, provided they were not abroad,
revelled in the stir her arrival always caused.

Nevertheless, her strong streak of common sense had
not allowed *her* coppery head to be turned. She knew
that, like anyone in the public eye, she was constantly
on trial, that she could not, for one instant, afford to

relax from her public image; and she worked conscientiously at putting herself across, liking people, wanting them to like her. It wasn't vanity, but part of the job; and it was not vanity which told her that the production team preferred her to Marcha. Gina was friendly with everyone, unpretentious, grateful for help and advice. She never played the 'star'.

'You mean you didn't *know* I'd be here?' Marcha sounded haughtily disbelieving.

'I had no idea,' Gina admitted to her cousin; and, to herself, that if she had known, she might not have been so ready to agree to Tod's proposition. She wasn't sure she relished having to work with Marcha again, if that was why the other girl was here. She couldn't forget her cousin's callous indifference, when . . .

'I can't think why Tod didn't tell you.' Marcha's eyes narrowed speculatively. 'Since it was his idea that you should train as my double.'

'As . . . as your double?' Gina's unease increased.

'Yes!' The other girl continued impatiently. 'What did you think this was in aid of? Some wretched secretary of his watches your programme every week, noticed this family likeness of ours. I needed a stand-in and she had to go and suggest you. I don't need to tell you I objected . . . strongly.'

'Marcha! I haven't the least idea what you're talking about.'

'You have, I presume, spent your time here training as as stuntwoman?' And, as Gina nodded, 'Filming is an expensive business. If a leading player falls ill, it holds up the work of hundreds of people, adds enormously to the cost. Illness can't be helped, but injury can, by employing a double to do the stuntwork.'

'I'm well aware of the function of doubles,' Gina returned. 'But just what are you trying to tell me?'

'That you're *my* stand-in, of course. Much as I
would have loved to do everything myself . . .'

'You?' Gina said ironically. 'Pull the other one!
You're the world's worst coward. It's like you to want
a stand-in. You don't care just *how* much other people
are injured do you, Marcha? Young, innocent people,
like . . .'

'Shut up! Shut up!' her cousin shouted furiously.
'Don't you dare to mention that incident here. Tod
knows nothing about it. I don't want you here, Gina,
and I shall tell Tod so. He'll have to get rid of you if he
wants to keep me.'

Dismay mingled with the growth of Gina's inward
anger. Tod had never actually said anything—oh, he'd
been too clever for that—but he had allowed her to gain
the impression that she was to star in his film.

'Of course there are other reasons, besides monetary
ones, why Tod wants to protect me,' Marcha broke in
on her cousin's thoughts. 'He couldn't bear to have me
hurt. His first wife was killed performing a stunt.'

'His *first* wife?' Gina said carefully.

Marcha laughed complacently.

'A bit premature of me, a slip of the tongue. It's not
generally known, but Tod and I will be getting married.
Probably when this film is in the can.'

'I see,' Gina said, and she thought she did. Her
former conclusions had been totally wrong. The barrier
between her and Tod had not been the shadow of
Maria Mantalini, but that of Marcha. No wonder Tod
had gone too far at times; he'd been using her as a
substitute for Marcha in more ways than one. What
would Marcha think if she knew that, she reflected
bitterly. But Gina would never stoop to tell her,
whereas, if the positions had been reversed . . .

'You haven't eaten your lunch,' Marcha pointed out
now.

'No . . . no, I haven't.' She pushed it away from her.

'Still it's just as well. I'm swimming this afternoon with Tod. It isn't wise to swim on a full stomach.'

'Oh I don't think you will be. Because I'm back a day earlier than he expected, Tod wants to run through the script with me. We play lovers in the film. Very appropriate, isn't it?' Marcha was smugly self-satisfied.

'Very appropriate!' Gina said drily, wondering if she had imagined the innuendo. Just how thoroughly would Tod and Marcha be following the script that afternoon? By all accounts they had been apart for a while. 'Since I seem to have some free time,' she continued, 'I think I'll make the most of it. Excuse me.'

She had reached the dining-room door, when Marcha recalled her, her tone acidly sweet.

'I suppose you didn't by any chance think you'd be playing this part?'

Gina's cheeks scorched.

'I see that you did!' Marcha wasn't speaking so sweetly now. 'But then dear Tod can be just a little unscrupulous in obtaining his ends. I shouldn't set your heart on any kind of part if I were you. Not after I've spoken to him.'

After her hectic morning, Gina had thought longingly of a restful afternoon. But now her wish was granted the empty hours no longer seemed desirable. Her mind was in a turmoil, varying emotions fighting to gain the upper hand. There was disappointment, downright chagrin in fact, that she was not to play the female agent in Tod's film. There was annoyance that Tod had not put her fully in the picture. Had he deliberately misled her, as Marcha had insinuated, or had it never occurred to him that she might make the wrong assumption? She wasn't really afraid, however, that Tod would dismiss her. By all accounts he'd known of Marcha's unwillingness to have her cousin as her stand-in, but he'd still gone ahead and hired her and she didn't think Tod was a man to see all his weeks of training go for nothing.

Uppermost was a dragging depression. Tod was going to marry Marcha. Despite the physical attraction that had flared between them, Gina stood no chance with him. The chemistry that she'd hoped might develop into something deeper was just that, chemistry. Tod *loved Marcha*. But Gina knew her cousin wasn't worthy of his love. Totally selfish, Marcha was incapable of making him happy. If only he knew about . . . But she could never be the one to tell him.

In this frame of mind, Gina knew she would never be able to rest and, on a sudden impulse, she turned aside to knock at the nursery door. It opened a fraction to reveal the anxious face of Sally, the nursemaid. But when she saw Gina, she opened the door fully, smiling her relief.

'It's you, miss. I'm always afraid . . .'

'That it might be kidnappers?' Gina followed the girl into the room. 'Were you working for Mr Fallon then?'

'When the second attempt was made, yes, miss. It was horrible. One man had a gun, and another had one of those horrible flick knives.'

'Where was this?'

'Out in the grounds, miss. I was walking Melanie in her baby buggy. She was smaller then, and it was before Mr Fallon had all those electric fences put round the walls.'

'What happened?'

'Luckily both Greg and Andy were around that day. They managed to disarm the men and throw them out, but it was a near thing.' The girl shuddered.

'Can I see Melanie?' Gina asked, glancing towards the closed door of an inner bedroom.

'Do you really want to be bothered, miss? You look rather tired if you don't mind me saying so. Melanie can be a real handful, very demanding.'

Gina smiled wryly. Melanie Fallon must have a lot of her father in her make up.

'Frankly, I'd welcome some sort of diversion,' she confessed. 'I'm a bit fed up right at this moment.'

'So's Melanie. That's why she's acting up. Ever since she heard that *she* was back.'

Gina didn't need to ask whom. That was obvious, since her encounter with Marcha.

The child was sitting in a window seat, looking down broodingly into the grounds. Here in the bedroom, as in the nursery, was every plaything a child might want; a rich man's child, yet the little figure was a pathetic one. She turned and, at the sight of Gina, her olive-complexioned face brightened and she beckoned imperiously.

'Come and sit here with me. I didn't think you'd *ever* come. No one else bothers, except Greg and Andy.'

'What about your father?' Gina tried to hide her disapproval. Didn't he ever make time to play with his small daughter?

'Sometimes,' Melanie admitted, 'but quite often he's too busy and when *she's* here, I don't want him to come, because *she* comes with him.'

Of course, as Tod's future wife, Marcha would need to get acquainted with his daughter. Gina frowned slightly. It was out of character. Normally Marcha had no time for children. In fact she had always claimed to detest them.

'Well, I'm not busy this afternoon,' she said in a deliberately cheerful tone. 'I'll play with you if you like. What shall we do?'

'What I'd *really* like,' Melanie said wistfully, 'is to go down there.' She pointed out into the grounds. 'Greg says the gardener's cat has kittens. Sally, do you think Daddy would let me have one, for my very own? It *would* be somebody to play with.'

Gina looked at Sally, her face expressing all that she

felt for the child's pathetic state of loneliness, and saw
her sympathy reflected in the nursemaid's face.

'We'll ask him about the kitten,' Sally promised, 'but
you know you're not allowed outside unless Greg or
Andy goes with us.'

'Oh, well!' The child was philosophical for one so
young; Gina would have expected tantrums. 'At least
I've got you! What's your name?' Gina told her. 'I like
that. It sounds Italian. I'm half-Italian,' she bragged as
she slid from the window seat. 'Did you know that, and
that my wicked grandpa wants to steal me?'

So Melanie knew that. Fancy allowing her to be
troubled by such fears; how could she ever have a
normal childhood?

'Don't worry,' Gina said comfortingly. 'Your daddy
would never let that happen.'

'Oh, I wouldn't mind,' the child said surprisingly. 'I
could go to Italy and meet all my relations. Then I'd
have plenty of people to play with. I'd rather live with
my grandpa, anyway, if Daddy's going to marry *her*.'

'You really will have to stop calling Miss Durrant
that!' Sally remonstrated. 'When she's your stepmother . . .'

'I *shan't* call her Mummy *or* Aunt Marcha!' Melanie
stamped one small foot. 'She's not my mummy or my
aunt and she'll be a *wicked* stepmother, I know she
will, much more wicked than my grandpa!' The childish
lips set mulishly, but they had a tendency to tremble.
Observing this Gina put an arm around the child's
shoulders.

'I'm sure your daddy won't let anyone be unkind to
you and we're not going to worry about it just now.
You never know, he might not get married.' She was
telling herself that as well as the child. The only
trouble was that, whereas Melanie's face brightened,
Gina could not believe so easily in her own optimism.
'Look, I can see Greg down there. Let's knock on the

window and ask him up. Perhaps he'll take us to see the kittens.'

Greg's delight was all too evident and Gina had an uncomfortable suspicion that most of his pleasure was derived from the prospect of her company.

'You haven't forgotten we have a date tonight?' he asked.

'I haven't forgotten,' Gina said, aware of Melanie's interested stare.

The cat and her kittens were housed in an unused wing of the stable block. Already the kittens were mischievous, ready to leave their mother. There were six of them in assorted colours.

'I shall have the black one,' Melanie announced.

The black kitten was a pathetic scrap, the smallest of the litter. It was not as boisterous as its brothers and sisters and Gina doubted whether it would thrive.

'Wouldn't you rather have one of the livelier, healthier ones?' she asked. 'What about the pretty little ginger one?'

But Melanie was stubborn, another trait which seemed to be inherited equally from mother and father, Gina reflected.

'No. This one's like me. He's lonely. The others don't play with him. I want him.'

She sat in the straw with the kitten in her lap, quite content to watch as the naughtier, more inquisitive ones climbed all over Gina, sticking like burrs to her slacks and sweater, licking her with tiny sandpaper tongues.

They were, all three of them, Melanie, Greg and Gina, still sprawled in the straw, and Greg was attempting to remove a stubborn kitten from the front of Gina's sweater, when Todd looked over the half door. They were all making so much noise with their talk and laughter that they hadn't heard his light tread, and Tod was able to stand, unobserved, for some minutes, his dark eyes unconsciously wistful at first as they surveyed the warm, attractive, almost domestic scene. His daughter, more dishevelled and grubby than he had ever seen her, yet also, somehow, happier, was clutching a kitten, while innumerable others seemed to be using Greg and Gina as an assault course.

Dishevelment suited Gina, he brooded. Her cheeks and eyes glowed with laughter. An emerald green sweater clung lovingly to her generous breasts and as Greg attempted to remove the kitten, his hand accidentally brushed against her lovely curves. Instantly, Tod felt within himself the stir of the other man's reaction, as he saw how Greg, his eyes involuntarily widening, movement arrested, looked at Gina.

She was not unaware either, he noticed. Her flushed face was in profile to Tod as she lifted her eyes to Greg's, and he saw her bite on her lip, a troubled little gesture. But then she was smiling again, pushing the other man's hands away.

'Better let me do that.'

'Gina!' Greg's husky voice carried to Tod's alert ears and his hands clenched at his sides. And, as Greg leant forward, his mouth seeking Gina's parted lips, Tod erupted into the loose-box.

'So there you are, Gina! I thought I made it quite clear that I wanted you down at the pool this afternoon. And after searching everywhere for you, what do I find? You, fraternising with one of my men; a man, furthermore,' he glared at Greg, 'who's supposed to be on duty; and I find my daughter, looking like a gutter brat.'

In one swift movement, he scooped Melanie from the straw, the kitten tumbling away. He thrust his daughter at Greg.

'Here! Get her back to the nursery. I'll talk to you and Sally later. As for you . . .' as Gina made to slip past him, 'I'll deal with *you* here and now.'

Greg's pleasant, rugged face was red with mingled

guilt and embarrassment, but Melanie proved more recalcitrant. She set up a heartbroken wailing.

'You've hurt my kitty. I want my kitty. *Gina* said I could have him.'

'I . . .' Gina began, then faltered into silence as she met Tod's glare.

'Be quiet, Melanie!' he roared. 'You're not having the damned thing. It's probably full of fleas. Greg, tell Sally that child's to have a bath immediately and her hair washed.'

'OK, Mr Fallon.' Greg paused in the doorway, his muscular arms easily restraining the threshing child. 'See you about seven then, Gina.'

'I'm looking forward to it!' she told him with deliberate enthusiasm.

Melanie's screams diminished into sobbing, and, as Greg departed with the child, there was silence in the stable, an ominous silence, broken only by the sound of breathing, Tod's deep and heavy with recent anger, Gina's fast and light with apprehension and indignation. Rather than wait for the predictable attack, she plunged into the offensive.

'You callous brute! There's nothing I hate worse than a man who's cruel to children and animals. Melanie was happy, really happy . . .'

'So was Greg, I noticed,' Tod snarled.

So that was what was eating him, because she'd defied his policy of non-fraternisation.

'We were *all* happy,' she retorted, 'until you came along.'

'I spend a fortune on two men's salaries just to see that my daughter comes to no harm and you . . .'

'She wasn't in any danger!' Gina snapped. 'Greg was here . . .'

'With his mind on other things.' The ginger kitten was still adhering to Gina's sweater and almost absently he reached out to pluck it away, but she retreated.

'Leave it alone and leave me alone.'

'I didn't hear you protesting so violently when Greg tried to come to your assistance.'

'No! Because he's my friend. You're only my employer and he hasn't tried to deceive me . . .'

'And *I* have?' Tod's heavy brows rose enquiringly.

'You know damned well you have! Oh, you were very clever. You never actually put it into words, but you must have known what I thought.'

'No,' sardonically, 'please enlighten me.'

'You didn't tell me I was just a stand in for Marcha Durrant, that I was to take all the risks, while she takes all the glory.'

'What touching family feeling. Marcha is your cousin.'

'Very distant, not distant enough for me.'

'Do I detect a note of female jealousy?'

'No, you do not! I wouldn't change places with Marcha if it meant my name in lights in Hollywood. She hasn't got a thing I want.' Except you, her heart mourned, but she kept her features strictly schooled.

'Yet you wouldn't have objected to her part in my film.' He had her there.

'I assumed, you led me to believe, it was my part.'

'Not at all,' he denied coolly. 'The subject was never discussed. I said nothing which could lead you to suppose anything so ridiculous. *You* play the lead in a major production? What acting experience have *you* had?'

It was an unanswerable question. He knew she had none. But she had a question for him.

'Why did you hire me when you knew Marcha objected so strongly? And now that she's back, do I get the sack?'

'Not at all,' he said calmly. 'Marcha is many things in my life, but she doesn't tell me how to make my films. And to return to the whole point of this conversation, why weren't you at the pool this afternoon?'

'Because,' she said witheringly, 'you were to be otherwise engaged.'

'Who said so?' he asked sharply.

'Marcha, of course.'

A look of palpable disbelief crossed his face.

'You've made it pretty clear that you've no natural affection for your cousin. Well, she told me you were a pretty cold fish. But don't you think it's rather despicable to lie about her, to blame *her* for your rebellious defiance?'

Gina opened her mouth, then closed it again. What was the use, she thought wearily. It was her word against Marcha's and it was pretty obvious who Tod was going to believe. But why had Marcha told Tod she, Gina, was cold? What was her cousin up to?

'Can I go now?' she asked.

'No! I haven't finished with you yet. I warned you, Gina, to stay away from the men in this outfit. Stay away from Greg Gibson! I want his mind on his job, not on your body . . .' a husky note crept into his voice, 'delectable though it may be. And since you obviously have no sense of responsibility, stay away from my daughter as well.'

Swift as a lance, the answer came back.

'Is that why *you* stay away from her? Because you don't have any responsibility towards her, other than as a provider of expensive, useless toys, as a gaoler. What about being a natural father for once, noticing that a child needs affection, company of her own age, or, failing that, a pet to love? Something warm, something living, that she can call her own.'

'Ah!' He scowled. 'I wondered when we'd get around to the cat, mangy, flea-ridden . . .'

'It is *not* mangy. Flea-ridden it may be, but fleas can be dealt with and Melanie loves it. Look at it, go on, look at it.' She picked up the black kitten and thrust it under his nose. 'Take notice for once of something lovable, something that doesn't mean money.'

His eyes flickered briefly over the kitten, then returned to her flushed, angry face, dropped to the tumultuous heaving of her breasts.

'I'd rather look at you,' he said softly, 'but then you know that, don't you? Did I say you couldn't act? I'm beginning to wonder!' Suddenly his hands erupted from his sides, clamped her upper arms and he shook her as he spoke. 'Dammit, Gina! Just how devious are you? Do you know, I wonder, just how effective your anger is, how magnificent it makes you look? I think you do. Can you assume it at will?'

'Anger? You think my anger's assumed?' she spat at him. 'Don't be so damned patronising. I don't need to pretend with you. You make me bloody, seething furious, with your arrogance, your high-handed ways, your inhumanity! And you had the neck to call *me* cold. You're Mr Iceberg himself.'

Suddenly the atmosphere about them was charged with an electricity that was not only that of anger, and other tempestuous emotions made Gina tremble. But this time she was determined she would not be disarmed, become putty in his hands. Boldly, she continued to outface him.

'Let go of me! I'm Marcha's stand-in, remember? She's back now, so you don't need a substitute, you can go and sate your sexual appetites on her!'

'While you do likewise with Greg, I suppose?' he snarled. 'Oh, I noticed your reference to a date, made in flagrant defiance of my orders.'

Once she would have denied vehemently that there was anything between herself and Greg other than mutual liking, but she knew that on Greg's side there was more and, besides, she felt annoyed, contrary.

'As I told you before, who I date is my business. And

since we're on the subject of free time, I want a whole day off next week.'

'For what purpose?' he snapped.

'To go and see someone I usually visit regularly. I haven't been able to go since I've been here.'

'Another boyfriend?'

'You could say that.' After all, Rusty certainly wasn't female.

'Greg not enough for you?' he taunted. 'And you talk about my sexual appetites! And if I refuse permission?'

'I'll go anyway.' She elevated the square, stubborn chin. 'It's important to me.'

With one finally exasperated, bruising grip of his hands, he released her, stood frowning down at her, his expression, she noted gleefully, one of frustrated exasperation.

'Can I go now?' she asked again, coolly.

'Yes, go! Go your own damn fool, pig-headed way. And here,' as she was about to turn on her heel, 'take this thing with you.' With one fluid movement he bent and scooped up the black kitten. 'Tell Greg to have the local vet check it over and clean it up. Then Melanie can have the blasted thing!' His manner was suddenly the awkward, endearingly sulky one of a small boy trying to make amends.

Good Lord, the man had a streak of humanity in him after all, Gina marvelled as she received the fluffy scrap from his hands.

In doing so, their fingers accidentally brushed and static shock seemed to spark through her. Damn it, would nothing ever quell this man's irritating effect upon her senses? To hide her agitation, she turned away with no word of acknowledgment for his unexpected concession and almost ran across the stableyard in search of Greg.

For the first time that day, she was glad she had accepted the security man's invitation to go out with him. She needed something, someone, *anyone* to take her mind off Tod Fallon. Why wouldn't the message her brain imparted infiltrate the rest of her, quell turbulent heart and traitorous body? The message that he belonged to Marcha.

'Where are we going?' she asked Greg, as they left Mallions that evening.

'Somewhere local, I'm afraid. Even on my evening off I'm still on call.' He patted his breast pocket. The unobtrusive bulge, Gina knew by now, was a personal alarm. 'If this thing starts, I have to get to a phone, or back to Mallions at the double.'

'I don't mind,' Gina assured him, as the gates opened to let Greg's fast sports car through. 'I'd prefer somewhere quiet and relaxing. Life's been pretty hectic lately.'

'Tod been driving you, hmm? Well, I expect you've guessed the reason? No need for me to keep my mouth shut, now that his "star" is back from her holidays ... two weeks late, I might add. No wonder he's been a bit testy. I for one don't blame him. I wouldn't trust that dame any further than I could kick her.'

'Oh?' Gina couldn't hide her curiosity.

'Proper little hot pants where men are concerned, our Marcha Durrant. At the moment she's satisfied with Tod, because he gave her her *entrée* into films. But if another, bigger director came along, I wouldn't give that,' Greg snapped his fingers, 'for Fallon's chances.'

'She gave me the impression,' Gina said, carefully casual—no one must ever know how it hurt—'that they'd be getting married after this film.'

'What!' Greg's sideways glance was sardonic. 'Haven't you figured Tod Fallon yet? No dame, however sexy, will ever get him to the altar again. Not after what happened to Maria. I reckon what passed for his heart was buried with that little Italian girl. No, he believes in loving 'em and leaving 'em. Marcha's lasted longer than most. By "love", I'm not referring to the emotion, you understand?'

'Oh, I understand all right!' Gina told him grimly.

'Made a pass at you, too, has he?' Greg sounded oddly fierce. 'First off we all reckoned you were the next in succession.'

Gina didn't want the conversation to take this personal turn. She directed her companion's thoughts back to her cousin.

'So you don't think his relationship with Marcha will last?'

'Not only that, we hope it won't. She's bad news. In fact, we all thought she'd walked out for good, but, like the bad penny she is, she's back.'

'Did they have a row?'

'Not exactly. Marcha's a dab hand at emotional blackmail. She can usually get her own way straight off. But Tod got pretty narked, when she refused to do her own stunting. He told her straight, more famous stars than she'll ever be managed without doubles. It was a near thing, I reckon, but she's got one advantage that she uses to good effect.'

'Oh?'

'Yeah! Her body. However mad Tod gets with her, one wiggle of that sexy little bottom and he's promising milady the earth; and this time it was her own stuntwoman.'

'I see.' Gina was silent, until the braking of the sports car disturbed the gravel frontage of a small, picturesque pub. So Marcha's hold on Tod was more precarious than her cousin had boasted. Not that it improved Gina's chances. She had no wish, anyway, to be one in a succession of short-lived affairs. She didn't like the picture Greg had painted for her of a man refusing ever again to be swayed by emotion, seeking only physical gratification, which swiftly palled.

'Hope you like pub food?' Greg asked, as he steered Gina into the bar.

The interior was in keeping with the exterior, white-walled and beamed. Twinkling brasses reflected subdued lamplight, pewter mugs hung above the bar and colourful Toby jugs were displayed at strategic points. They sat in a secluded corner on a padded bench semicircling an oak table.

The food was as good as a first-class restaurant. They chose succulent steaks with a side salad and Gina could not resist a generous slice of Black Forest gateau. As she deprecated her weakness, Greg smiled a disclaimer.

'You've no need to worry about your figure, Gina.' His gaze was openly admiring and his hand patted her thigh in a proprietary gesture, which she found she disliked. 'Not like Marcha. That one'll run to seed well before she's forty.' He broke off. 'Talk of the devil! Look who's here.'

Gina turned in her seat, dismayed to see Tod and Marcha entering the room, Tod helping Marcha to remove her coat. The bar room was too small for Greg and Gina to escape notice and in any case Greg was already lifting his hand in a lazy gesture of welcome. It was inevitable that the other couple should join them, though Marcha didn't look any more pleased than Gina felt.

'So you're back!' Greg observed to Marcha, as Tod went to the bar to order drinks. 'How was Italy?'

'Italy?' Marcha stared haughtily at him. 'What *are* you talking about? I was in France.'

'Funny.' Greg drawled. 'Steph and Debbie were in Italy a couple of weeks ago. They said they saw you.'

'Then they were mistaken,' Marcha said shortly.

Gina wondered if Marcha was lying. Had her extended holiday been connected with another man, another film director perhaps? Was Marcha two-timing Tod? Gina found herself hoping so, hoping Tod would find out. And what good would that do you, she asked herself cynically. You know you're not prepared to join the long line of 'has beens' in Tod's life.

Tod returned with their drinks and conversation became general, mostly about the film they would shortly be shooting.

'How's Gina shaping up?' Marcha asked Tod, as if Gina wasn't present. 'Is she fully trained?' Now she darted a sweet smile at Gina, a smile which Gina knew to be utterly false.

'No,' Tod was saying, 'but we can start work on the early stages of the film. Her tuition can go on concurrently. Making a horse fall won't present too much of a problem. Gina is an excellent horsewoman and Theresa already has a trained animal. It's just a matter of horse and rider practising together.'

Marcha's eyes had narrowed slightly at the mention of Theresa.

'You've been over to the stables while I've been away?'

Gina sensed her cousin's jealousy and suspicion. *Had* Theresa been one of Marcha's predecessors, or was the other girl afraid the stable owner might succeed her?

'Naturally we've been to Theresa's. You know she possesses the only suitable facilities.'

'Oh, Gina went with you?' The obvious relief in Marcha's tone wasn't very flattering. As if Marcha felt that Gina presented no competition.

'That was the purpose of the exercise.' Tod's manner was abrupt, almost absent. He didn't look at Marcha as he spoke. Instead, his eyes seemed to be fixed somewhere between Greg and Gina, or rather where the space between them should have been; for, their meal finished, Greg had moved closer on the leather bench-seat and now his arm was draped about her shoulders, his thigh pressed to hers; and Gina, though his proximity left her unmoved, permitted his touch, deliberately armouring herself against her vulnerability to Tod.

'Well, I guess we'll leave you folks to eat in peace,' Greg said, as a waitress brought the other couple's meal.

'Going straight back to Mallions?' Tod enquired casually.

'No. Thought we might take a drive around first,' Greg said. 'Gina hasn't had much chance to view the scenery. You've kept her nose pretty close to the grindstone since she's been here.'

'Actually I have been in Buckinghamshire before,' Gina said, 'but further south. I'd love a guided tour of this area.'

The countryside was quietly undulating, soft slopes of grass, woodland flung here and there in masses. Villages dotting the landscape added to the general peaceful aspect of the wide sweeps of green hills and valleys. They drove around for about an hour. Then, as it began to get too dark to appreciate the scenery, Greg turned the car for home.

'It's still early,' he said. 'Care for a nightcap?'

'A strictly non-alcoholic one then,' Gina said. 'I'm not a great drinker, except for the occasional glass of wine with a meal.'

'Whatever you like. You won't mind if I have a beer? I'm no toper. I wouldn't hold on to this job for long if I were. We have to be on the *qui vive* the whole time, but I do like the odd half pint.'

'Do you think Mantalini will try again?' Gina asked, as they sipped their drinks in Greg's comfortable sitting-room.

'Who knows? He's an old man now. Maria died three years ago. How long can you go on feeling anger, wanting revenge? It seems a pity for the kid to be deprived of her only grandparent and vice versa.' He put his beer mug down. 'But we didn't come here to talk about Tod's problems.'

'I didn't know the subject was taboo,' she said lightly, her intuition ahead of him in his next move.

'What I meant, as you very well know, is that we should be talking about us.' He came to sit on the side of her chair.

'Greg!' Gina thrust his arm away, speaking pleasantly but firmly. 'Don't get any ideas, please. Don't ruin a nice evening. There is no "us". We had a date, a friendly one, nothing more.'

'Aw, come on. You weren't so discouraging back there at the pub.'

'That was different. We were in public. I didn't want a scene. We're alone now and I can tell you, I don't play about, Greg.'

'Depends on what you call playing about.' Greg sounded annoyed now. 'I call it playing about to give a guy the "come on" in public and the cold shoulder in private.'

'I'm sorry if you've misunderstood me,' Gina said quietly. 'I never intended . . .'

'No?' Greg said, then, slowly, bitingly, 'no, you didn't intend to give *me* the wrong idea. It was Tod, wasn't it? I noticed the way he was watching us. Maybe you two have got a thing going, in spite of Marcha. Maybe you were trying to make him jealous.'

'Don't be ridiculous!' It was too near to the truth for comfort.

'No, Gina! I don't like to appear ridiculous, or to be made to look ridiculous.' There was a menacing undercurrent in Greg's voice now. The big amiable man had disappeared and in his place was one slighted ego. 'Which is why I intend to get out of the evening at least what I put into it.'

Threats of that kind left Gina unperturbed.

'I think you're confusing me with some other type of girl,' she told him. 'I don't "pay" for my entertainment "in kind".'

'Maybe you haven't in the past. But if you get involved with Fallon, you'll have to change your principles. And right now you're going to get some practice. And it's no use struggling,' as he grabbed her in a clumsy bear hug. 'You're no match for me.'

'Greg!' Desperately Gina twisted her face from side to side. 'Please don't do this. You'll be sorry when you're sober. I don't want to fall out with you. I'd much rather we stayed friends.'

'If you want to stay friends, then co-operate,' he growled. 'Don't forget, you angled for this date . . .'

'I didn't, I . . .'

But his mouth was grinding hers into silence and during that silence, Gina made up her mind. As he stopped to draw a shuddering breath, she warned him.

'Greg, if you don't like to appear ridiculous, let me go this instant, or that's just what's going to happen.'

'What could you possibly do? Come on now,' placatingly, 'we'll take it more slowly if you like . . .'

One minute he was standing straight, an arm holding her firmly, his free hand attempting to cup her breast, the next moment his head was lower than his heels on his way to lying flat on the floor. He shook his head, blinked, then made to get up.

'Stay there!' she told him.

Neither of them heard the door open just as Greg, ignoring her warning, rose and made a dive at her. One leg and one hand arrested his progress in such a way that he tripped and fell heavily once more. This time the breath was knocked from his body and he lay prone, gasping.

'Judo, by God! You play rough with your boyfriends!'

Gina whipped round to see Tod leaning in the doorway, his expression unfathomable.

'Fallon!' Greg had recovered himself somewhat. 'What the hell? This is a private room,' he growled as he crawled painfully to his feet.

'A private room for your own use, yes. But it is under my roof, I would remind you, and not a place to entertain your floosies!'

'How dare you call me a . . .' Gina began, but Tod cut in as if she hadn't spoken.

'You're fired, Gibson.'

'But . . .'

'You heard me. You're fired.' He turned on Gina. 'And you . . . get the hell out of here.'

'Are you firing me, too?' She held herself proudly erect.

'Don't tempt me! Is that what you want? To leave with Gibson?'

'N-no, of course not,' she faltered, 'I . . .'

'Then get out of here. Get to your own quarters.'

But in all fairness she couldn't leave without attempting to put things right. However annoyed she was with Greg, she'd had no reason to fear for her safety and she hadn't meant to lose him his job.

'Greg, I'm sorry. I wouldn't have had this happen . . .' Her words faltered away as the big man turned his back on her. Tod continued to stare at her implacably, threateningly. There was nothing she could do right now but obey him.

CHAPTER SEVEN

'Tod?' Gina studied his unapproachable profile as they drove out towards the riding stables next morning. She still felt guilty about Greg's dismissal, because she *had* been using the other man for her own ends.

He hadn't answered her and she tried again.

'Tod . . . about Greg . . .'

'*What* about him?' he snapped, with more ferocity than she had expected.

'Did you really have to fire him? I feel . . .'

'Yes?' His profile was still granite-like. 'Just what *do* you feel for Greg, Gina? I'd be interested to know.'

She ignored his ill-humour and persevered.

'I feel you were too hard on him. He wasn't behaving any worse than . . . than . . .' She stopped abruptly, aware of treading on dangerous ground.

'Yes?' he enquired ominously. 'Go on!'

'All right! I will.' She reacted defiantly to his tone. 'His behaviour wasn't any worse than yours! At least he was only trying to kiss me. Whereas you . . . you . . .' Again she could not go on and swiftly she changed tack. 'When I first arrived, you said if my presence interfered with anyone else's work, it would be me that got fired. Why didn't you . . .'

'Why didn't I fire you? Use your head! Do you think I want all your training to be wasted?'

'But surely that's less important than Melanie's safety?'

'Why should you worry about her? I didn't think you "career" women were overfond of children.'

Gina winced. His words had struck her a body blow. But then Tod couldn't know how she longed to have

122

children, couldn't know that happiness was forever denied her.

'I'm very fond of children,' she told him now, 'and Melanie is a darling. That's why I believe you should think again about firing Greg.'

'Don't worry.' He sounded almost weary. 'You're not losing your boyfriend. I've told him he can stay.'

Gina's face broke into a smile of relief, but to the man, glancing sideways at her, its apparent radiance held other connotations.

'Perhaps now,' he said brusquely, 'we could concentrate on business?' And Gina realised that, for the last five minutes, they had been parked in Theresa's stableyard and she hadn't even noticed, so intent had she been upon the subject of their discussion.

'Today you're going to meet The Clown. He's a horse.' A wry smile answered her look of surprised enquiry. 'Theresa christened him that when she found he was a "natural" at playing the fool, ideal material for a "falling" horse. Certain horses are kept for certain stunts, simply because they have an aptitude for them. The Clown is a "faller"!'

'The Clown has been taught to fall when required,' Tod explained, 'but even so, his rider has to learn to control him.'

'It seems rather cruel,' Gina said doubtfully, as they watched Theresa saddling up, preparatory to giving a demonstration.'

'Not at all. Such horses are valuable and treated with great care. Everything is taught by kindness. All you need is time, patience and plenty of sugar!'

Though he had proved an apt pupil from the first, Tod told Gina, the gelding's training had been very gradual. At first his foreleg had been bent and tied with a rope or bandage around the knee. The extra large saddle he wore was capable of taking a considerable weight of equipment and had a hole just below the pommel. During early training, a lunge rope passing through the hole had been attached to the right side of the bit, used in conjunction with a curb chain under the jaw.

'When the trainer pulls on the rope,' Tod told her, 'if the horse allows himself to fall easily to the left, then he's likely to make a good faller. First falls are made indoors, with the horse standing still and the floor covered in deep sawdust, so that there's no danger of injury.'

'Suppose a horse does hurt itself?'

'It would hold up his training for a considerable period of time because, for quite a while, he'd refuse to fall again. When the horse has taken to falling readily on the lunge rope, the rope is replaced by a rein, as now. Watch Theresa.'

The slight girl had mounted. She demonstrated The Clown's accomplishments, bringing her mount down from a walk, then a trot and finally at the canter.

'Now we come to your training,' Tod said. 'This particular stunt is very demanding. As his rider, you're responsible for the fall being made in exactly the right place, for giving him the correct signal at the correct moment. In effect, you're responsible for the horse's safety as well as your own.'

Gina was a little nervous at first, not so much for herself, but that she should not harm an obviously valuable animal. But Theresa was coolly competent and since Tod had wandered off, leaving the two girls together, she felt less pressure and by the end of the session was giving quite a good account of herself.

'Give her a week,' Theresa told Tod, when he returned, 'and she should be ready to go. Fortunately, you've picked yourself an excellent horsewoman.' She smiled at Gina in a friendly fashion and Gina found herself liking the other girl.

Next morning, Tod handed over the keys of his car.

'Think you can get yourself over to Theresa's for the rest of your lessons?'

'What will you be doing?' Gina felt a stab of disappointment. She had enjoyed her early morning drives with Tod, able to pretend for a while that he was hers.

'We start filming today. We'll work on Marcha's scenes, the close-ups, and then, when you're ready to go, we'll take the "stand-in" shots.'

In her absence, would they also be shooting the love scenes between Marcha and Tod? Gina hoped so. She hoped fervently that they would all be completed before she was expected to attend the filming sessions. She didn't want to actually see Marcha in Tod's arms; imagining it was bad enough.

For the rest of that week, she travelled alone, returning to Mallions each day, sore and weary, but with a growing sense of achievement. She was becoming more and more confident of her ability to do what was asked of her. She saw little of Tod or Marcha. If they were not filming, they seemed to be dining out. Greg was coldly civil whenever she encountered him and she was sorry their easy cameraderie was gone.

Thus, feeling a little lonely, Gina began spending her spare time in the nursery.

'I wonder,' Sally said one evening, rather diffidently, 'if you'd mind being on your own with Melanie. I have the offer of a date and I'd rather like to accept.'

'Of course you must go,' Gina said at once. 'I'd love to babysit.'

'Do you think we ought to ask Mr Fallon's permission first?'

'We can't. He's out himself. But in any case, I don't see why he should object, as long as there's someone with Melanie. Andy's on duty outside tonight, isn't he?'

So it was arranged, and Gina had the satisfaction of playing with the child, giving her her tea, bathing her

and reading a bedtime story until she fell asleep. She
turned the light down, barely a glimmer retained just in
case Melanie woke. There was no reason now why she
should not return to the outer room and read her own
book. But somehow it was very peaceful, sitting here in
the dim light, watching the child's lovely little face
tranquil in sleep, hearing the even tenor of her
breathing. Seated in a low chair beside the bed, Gina
leant over Melanie, her expression rapt, her eyes
wistful. How she would have loved a daughter just like
this.

So engrossed was she in her silent worship that she
did not hear the soft opening of the door that
communicated between nursery and bedroom. But then
awareness of another presence in the room made her
start. She knew at once who it was, every nerve end told
her. After Tod had assured himself of his daughter's
well-being, he beckoned Gina to follow him into the
outer room.

'What the hell,' he demanded, 'are you doing here?
Where's Sally?'

'She had the chance of an evening out, so I
volunteered to babysit.'

'I suppose,' he said sarcastically, 'that it never
occurred to either of you that, as Sally's employer, my
permission might be sought?'

'Yes, it occurred to us,' Gina said evenly, 'but since
you were out yourself, presumably with Marcha, it
wasn't possible to consult you. It seemed a pity for
Sally to miss her chance, just because you're always out
enjoying yourself. And I'm quite capable of looking
after Melanie.'

He moved to shut the door between the two rooms,
then returned, studying her appraisingly.

'You puzzle me,' he said at last.

'Oh?' she returned lightly. 'In what way?'

'This . . . this "thing" you seem to have about your

cousin. Don't think I haven't noticed your subtle denigration of her. Yet she never has anything but good to say of you.'

Gina's lip curled. How easily men were deceived by a lovely face, and of course Marcha was a consummate actress, by profession and by nature.

'Except apparently, that I'm "frigid".'

'That,' he said drily, 'was in the nature of a recommendation as far as I was concerned. She knows my views on fraternisation and she said you'd hardly be a threat to any of my crew, since you'd turned violently against all men; that probably you should never have married in the first place, since you weren't the domesticated or the romantic type.'

'Well thank you, Marcha!' Gina exclaimed. 'As a recommendation that takes the biscuit. Or was it a recommendation? It sounds to me as if she was more afraid that your attention might wander in her absence. Obviously she's not blind to your weaknesses.'

To accuse a man like Tod of any weakness was a dangerous thing to do, a provocation to retaliation. Gina recognised the danger signals in the tightening of his lips, the hardening of his eyes.

'Are you blind to your weaknesses, Gina?' he asked softly. He moved to the outer door of the nursery and, scarcely believing her eyes, she saw him turn the key in the lock.

'W-what are you doing? I don't know what you mean.' Unfortunately, she did and the knowledge turned her knees to water.

'Oh, you know very well, Gina. It seems Marcha was mistaken. With your own sex you may be able to keep up your act, but not with a man, a real man. I don't know anything about your husband, whether or not he was capable of plumbing your depths, but I know I am. I've come very close to it once or twice and now I'm tempted to go all the way.'

'No! You . . . you won't. I shan't let you. I'll . . .'

'You'll what? Throw me over your shoulder as you did Greg? Now that puzzles me, too! You've had plenty of opportunities, Gina, but you didn't take them. Is it possible you didn't really want to discourage *me*? Why didn't you use your unarmed combat skills?'

'I . . . I didn't think it would be any use,' she improvised. 'You said you'd been a stuntman. I . . . I thought your skills would be far more advanced than mine.'

'They are, as it happens. But I still don't believe you. I know women, Gina. You're not as immune to me as you'd have me believe. It's there in the way you talk about your cousin in relation to me. I believe you're jealous, not just because she has the lead in my film but because . . .'

'Because she's your mistress? Never!' Gina said vehemently. 'I'll never lower myself to be that to any man. If ever I were to trust one of your sex again, which I doubt, it would be marriage or nothing. Marcha may have the morals of an alley cat, but they don't run in the family.'

'No?' he enquired softly. 'Then how would you describe your undoubtedly receptive reactions to my lovemaking?'

'Lovemaking? Is that what you call it? I'd call it good old-fashioned lust. Oh, I won't deny you know precisely how to arouse a woman's baser instincts to match your own, and I am only human.'

'Yes, I know how to arouse you, Gina, and it's a very pleasurable experience. But I wouldn't call your instincts base, just natural. Especially in view of your alleged long abstinence.'

It was a warm night, but she knew that was not responsible for the prickles of nervous perspiration bedewing her skin. His eyes were fixedly regarding her breasts and she knew that the thrust of them against the

thin material of her summer dress was betraying her
body's immediate reaction to him, to his words. Her
instinct was to step backwards, but there was nowhere
to retreat.

To relieve their nervous dryness, she licked her lips,
tried to avoid his gaze, but his eyes held hers. His were
amused, yet dark, too, with something else, something
physically frightening yet, at the same time, infinitely
exciting. Like a wild creature charmed by its predator,
she was unable to move as he reached out and touched
the soft creamy flesh exposed by the elasticated, boat-
shaped neckline of her dress.

'You're warm, Gina,' he murmured, 'warm and
living. What was it you said about everyone needing
something warm and living to hold?'

'I was talking about Melanie and . . . and the kitten.'
But she was helpless to push his hand away as it
continued its investigation.

He moved closer, both of his hands now employed in
stretching the neckline until it slid down, exposing her
shoulders, the swell of her breasts. Slowly, so slowly, his
head bent over her, then his mouth tasted and savoured
her skin, sending tremors of sensation through her,
arousing a desire to know more of his sensual expertise.

'I've found myself thinking about you a lot just
lately, Gina,' he murmured, 'imagining what it would
be like to make love to you fully.' His voice grew
throatier. 'Not just once, but day after day.'

If he only knew it, her thoughts had paralleled his
often, imagining such moments as this, moments,
however, of genuine emotion, of commitment, which
could be carried without shame to their natural
conclusion. *This* could not, must not.

His fingers at the nape of her neck drew her nearer to
him.

'Can you imagine it, Gina?' His voice was seductive,
evocative of the picture he painted. 'I know you can.

You, naked, in my arms, both of us naked. It so nearly happened once, didn't it? I touched your body, felt it come alive, but then I drew back, fool that I was. For a while I had this crazy idea that I was wrong about you, that you were worthy of something better, that you weren't for me or for any man on a casual basis. But I should have known better, shouldn't I? You wanted me then, you would have let me possess you, and I threw away my opportunity. Can you imagine how many times I've regretted that? But I'm not going to throw away my chance this time. Why should I when there's been Greg! And then there's this man you want to visit. I can't speak for him, of course, but I know Greg. I think I can promise you I'd be more subtle, more sensitive.'

She shook her head. He was wrong, horribly wrong in his insinuations and yet, bemused, still she stared into his eyes, unaware how hers registered her conflicting emotions. The recent, searing contact of his mouth against her shoulders had brought all the sensuality of her own nature into leaping life. He took advantage of her immobility, covering her mouth with his, parting her lips with consummate ease, the pressure of his warm and firm, erotically evocative.

Unable to restrain herself from following instincts she had long wished to indulge, she allowed her hands to glide up over Tod's broad shoulders, then over his neck, until her fingers were lost in the crisp, dark hair, a delicious, tactile experience. Meanwhile, he plundered her mouth with an expertise that made her whole body tremble furiously.

When the kiss ceased, it was all she could do to remain standing. Indeed, if it had not been for the support of his arms, she doubted she would have done so. His voice was warm, seductive.

'You want me, Gina, don't you?'

Helplessly, she shook her head, made an attempt to

pull away, but it was a feeble effort at best. She felt limp, boneless, and she could sense his triumphant awareness of her pliancy.

This time the pressure of his lips was harder as he sought to force a verbal as well as a physical acknowledgment from her, and she knew this was serious. He wasn't playing with her. His body proclaimed all too surely its own arousal, evidence of a very powerful and unmistakable physical need, and for the first time she began to realise that he did intend to appease it.

Her body grew warmer still as the blood heated and flowed more rapidly in her veins, while pulses hammered a minor accompaniment to her heart. There was no resistance in her, her total concentration was upon her senses, their crying needs. Too often her body had awakened to Tod's, too often been denied. Now he had no need to force her lips apart. They opened to him willingly, her tongue duelling frantically with his. Her hands clasped vicelike about his neck, as if they would never release him, her body stirred and pressed against him in deliberate provocation, making its own plea for satisfaction.

In answer, he pushed her down upon the settee, his weight upon hers a glorious, temporary appeasement of her wanting, but not for long. It was not enough. As his lips, his hands made tormenting trails over her body, she tensed against him, small husky groans in her throat protesting against his procrastination, urging him to release the pent-up dam of their mutual longing. Never, not even with Tod himself, had she experienced such violent, such painful surges of desire, feelings so strong that they obliterated all reason, all promptings of common sense, so that nothing mattered but that they should reach the natural harmony of final consummation.

It was the squeak of the communicating door that

broke across what no other force could have destroyed.
Melanie's bedroom door. This was no scene for a child
to witness. Abruptly they were apart, each thankful for
the temporary dazzlement in the child's eyes as she
came from the half-light of her room into the brightness
of the nursery.

'Gina, where's my kitten? I want him.'

'Sally took him down to the kitchen for his supper,'
Gina explained gently. To Tod, *sotto voce*, she said, 'We
thought you might not approve of him sleeping on her
bed.'

'Oh.' He shrugged impatiently and she knew
frustrated desire was still riding him, as it did her. 'If
she wants the animal let her have it. I'll go down and
get the damned thing.'

Gina guessed that he needed the excuse, time to bring
himself under control. As for herself, she concentrated
her attention on the child, drawing her into her arms,
leaning her cheek against the dark, curly hair. If only
this were her own child, she held ... hers and Tod's, the
outcome of their impassioned lovemaking. Such
intensity of feeling as they had known here this evening
would surely have resulted in ... Then she remembered,
remembered that such a thing could not be for her,
ever, with any man. Her face crumpled suddenly and
she felt the sting of bitter tears.

When Gina had realised how Keith had deceived her,
the traumatic shock had precipitated a miscarriage,
followed by the shattering intelligence that, for her,
there were unlikely to be more pregnancies.

For a long while before and after her divorce, Gina
had been low in health and spirits, too numb to care.
Grief for the child that might have been brought its
own, blessed, concomitant paralysis of thought. Only
later, when her physical strength began to return, did
she realise the depths of her hurt, the psychological
damage caused by the loss of her most valuable

feminine attribute. She hadn't realised until then just how much her confidence in her own femininity had buoyed her up in her career. Now she felt only half a woman, uncertain of her identity.

Returning, the kitten tucked under his arm, Tod paused on the threshold, his breath catching in his throat, all the measures he had taken to cool his feverish wanting undone by the sight before him.

How lovely she was, how lovely and how desirable. There was that family resemblance to Marcha and yet, somehow, disturbingly, she wasn't like her. And she sat there, holding his child, as if it were the most natural thing in the world that she should do so . . . his child! He felt his breath exhale raggedly. What sort of children would they produce, he and Gina, if ever . . . Then, as Gina had done, he crushed the thought. Never again, he vowed, never again. Those who loved got hurt. When Maria had died, he'd sworn always to keep a part of himself to himself; any hurt, therefore, would be minimal, easily shaken off. Never again would he submit mind and heart, as well as body, to the toll love took.

And now, here he was, almost wallowing in unwanted sentimentality, just because a lovely woman, whom he desired, nursed his child. He moved, cleared his throat and the little tableau was disturbed; but as Gina looked up, he caught the unmistakable glint of tears on her cheeks and all his resolutions wavered. He was beside her in an instant.

'What is it, Gina? Tell me, what is it?'

'N-nothing. At least . . .' She could not quell the little sob that rose in her throat. 'It was just that . . . sitting here with Melanie, it brought home to me all that I'm missing . . . a . . . a child of my own.' Her throat closed up. She could say no more. She couldn't find the words to tell him of her deepest unhappiness, that she could never bear a child.

So she was regretting the past, was she? Tod thought grimly. A few years ago, according to Marcha, she'd refused her husband's pleas that she lead a domesticated life, so he'd left her for a woman willing to bear his children. Yet despite this knowledge, Tod found himself unable to harden his heart against her. His arms encircled them both, Gina and the now sleeping child.

'Never mind, my love,' he whispered, 'it's not too late. You're still young.' He did not see the despairing shake of her head, the lips that shaped the word 'never' as he took Melanie from her arms and carried the child back to bed.

When he returned, he found Gina talking to Sally, her face as composed as if she had never shed those tears.

'Yes, thank you, miss,' Sally was saying. 'I had a lovely evening at the cinema at Aylesbury. Oh, Mr Fallon,' as she noticed him on the threshold of the two rooms, 'I hope you didn't mind, but . . .'

'Not a bit,' he said brusquely. 'I'm afraid we've all tended to take you for granted. I'm sure Miss Darcy will sit for you again?' He looked at Gina.

'Oh . . . oh yes,' she whispered, head suddenly downbent. But could she bear to do this again, expose her still vulnerable heart to the ecstatic agony of watching over another woman's child? But Melanie was also Tod's child; in holding Melanie, she held, too, a part of Tod, a very important part. She raised her head, eyes brilliant with yet more tears, but steadily fixed on his. 'I'd like that,' she said.

He steered her from the room and she went with him blindly, for the stupid tears would not let her see where she walked. On the darkened landing, he drew her into his arms again.

'I'll give you five minutes,' he whispered, his body trembling against hers, 'then I'll come to your room.'

Oh no. No. Give me the strength to resist, to refuse him, she pleaded inwardly.

'Gina?' His voice was questioning as he lifted her chin, endeavouring, in the gloom, to see her expression.

'No, Tod. Please. I . . . I'd rather you didn't.'

'Not tonight?' There was infinite tenderness in his voice, patience. 'Then some other night, darling, please?'

'Not tonight, not ever.' She tried to make her voice strong. 'I've told you before, I don't . . . don't . . .'

'This wouldn't be a casual affair, Gina.' His tone was sincere and she trembled anew. What was he trying to say? 'No one night stand. I swear to you, there'd be no other woman in my life but you.' It sounded like the prelude to a proposal of marriage and yet . . . Had he said those same words once to Marcha? 'Let me love you, Gina.'

'In what capacity?' she whispered.

He caught her to him anew. 'As my love, of course, my *dearest* love.'

'What the French call a *chère amie*, I suppose,' she said bitterly. 'No, Tod!' Sure now of her ground, she withdrew herself from his arms. 'I'm sorry, but no. Good night.' With an effort that cost all her will-power, she made herself turn and walk away from him towards her own room, head and shoulders erect. But she could not prevent herself turning briefly, her hand on the latch, to see him still standing there, watching her.

She saw him start eagerly towards her, as though he believed her to have relented, and with a swift movement she was inside her room, the door locked behind her. For a moment she stood listening, trembling, as his footsteps advanced, paused, were motionless for a long, long time. Then she heard a sigh, a deep-hearted one, as if it came from the very depths of his being, before he moved on.

Only then could she relax, sagging, almost tottering

to her bed where she threw herself face down, muffling the crying that felt as if her heart must break.

For Gina, her work began in earnest next day and she was glad of the tiring, sometimes actually painful activity that would render her body immune to all other sensations.

A grim-faced Tod greeted her, spoke to her as he did to any other member of his crew and, though she knew she ought to be relieved not to have any reminders of his softer moods, her heart was sore.

They were to begin making the linking shots, from where Marcha was seen mounting a horse, her expression of fear and distaste masked from the camera, until she was discovered, face down, supposedly having fallen with her horse. The ground over which Gina must gallop had been broken up and covered with shredded peat and other shock-absorbent materials on which the horse and rider would fall.

At first she had merely to take The Clown over the course he was to run, not only for the benefit of the director, Tod, and his cameramen, but also to rehearse the run for herself. The actual fall itself would not be practised, though Gina had been warned that she might have to do it several times with the cameras turning before Tod and his crew were satisfied with the result.

To Gina's surprise, Tod came over before the actual 'take' and uncertainly she wondered if the expression in his dark eyes was what it seemed to be, anxiety.

'All right?' he asked curtly. 'Not afraid?'

She shook her head, tightening her lips to quell their trembling. Not of fear; it was the light pressure of his hand on her back as she mounted which had been enough to disturb her hard-won equilibrium. For a moment her green eyes tried desperately to fathom the meaning of his.

It had taken Gina a while during training sessions to

get used to all the special equipment, the personal padding, the falling stirrups. These latter consisted of leather pouches, made so the rider's feet could be removed from them instantly without any risk of being dragged along the ground. Her elbows and knees were well protected. Her collarbones she must shield as she fell by folding her arms across them. Some riders wore close fitting jockey helmets, but in this case it was essential that her long, flowing red hair be visible.

'This time then?' he said, still looking up at her, and now there was no mistaking the agony in his eyes. *He was afraid, for her*, as she had been afraid in the past for so many others. Intuitively, from her own experience, she knew he would rather be up here, taking the risks himself, instead of watching her take them.

'I'll be all right,' she said quietly.

'OK, then. But for God's sake, watch your head when you fall. Cameras? Ready to follow? Take him away then.'

Gina urged The Clown forward. Faster and faster the gelding galloped as he approached the prepared stretch and Gina drew a deep breath, concentrating her mind totally on everything she had learned. One mistake now could spell disaster. As she reached the point of fall, she removed her left foot from the stirrup, at the same time thrusting her right leg out straight, and pulled hard on the right rein. As she felt The Clown beginning to fall to the left, she made sure *her* left leg was well clear of the horse's body and began her own fall towards the prepared ground.

As she lay there, slightly winded in spite of all her precautions, she heard pounding footsteps, then Tod was prone beside her on the ground, turning her over, his face inches from hers, his eyes anxiously scanning her face.

'Gina?' he asked urgently. 'Are you all right? When you didn't move, I thought . . .'

Bewildered, shaken by his proximity, his urgency, she stared into the bronzed features that meant so much to her.

'I thought I wasn't supposed to move,' she said, 'until . . .'

He swore then and a look of fury crossed his face.

'Did no one tell you we'd filmed the rest of that damned sequence, days ago? The cameras cut just now, as soon as you hit the ground. I thought . . . My God, I thought . . .'

For a moment she thought he would actually haul her into his arms, as he had done on the last occasion when he thought she'd been in danger, but then he seemed to recollect their surroundings, their audience. Instead, he hauled her to her feet and began walking her back.

'OK. Break for lunch,' Tod called, as they aproached the little group of technicians and actors. From the evidence of her pursed lips and flaring nostrils, Gina deduced that Marcha had not liked Tod's all too obvious concern for her stand-in. She heard her cousin's fluting voice deprecating people who couldn't remember the easiest instructions.

For the next two or three days, Gina was in constant demand. There were more riding scenes; swimming. Gina had to fly the little Cessna and this time she was aware of Tod's tension before she even took off. Something prompted her, an instinct which she swiftly regretted, to pass close to him en route to the aircraft and murmur,

'Don't worry, Tod. I'll be OK.'

He met her green compassionate gaze with an icy stare.

'No reason why you shouldn't be!' She felt chilled by his rebuff. Yet why shouldn't he rebuff her presumption? After all, if she did crash and kill herself, it would mean nothing to him except a temporary inconvenience, a delay in filming.

After five days of continuous stunting, Gina rebelled, demanding her day off, pointing out that she hadn't had one since she'd been at Mallions. At first she thought Tod was going to refuse.

'I suppose you want to visit this other, mysterious boyfriend of yours?' And, as she didn't answer, merely waited silently, 'Oh, do what you like! Take the Mini. I can't spare the Rolls today.'

As the vast gates of the estate opened and closed behind her, Gina had the sensation of one escaping from prison. It was as if a weight lifted from her; and yet she knew it was only a temporary reprieve from a life sentence. Under different circumstances she would be a voluntary inmate, if only Tod returned her love. She wouldn't mind spending the rest of her life behind iron gates and electrified fences with him and Melanie. But the invitation to do so would never be issued.

To banish these fruitless thoughts, she gave all her concentration to her driving and pressed on, her foot hard down, towards Aylesbury and beyond . . . to Stoke Mandeville.

'Hallo, Rusty!'

There was an instant's silence before the wheelchair turned on its axis, its occupant staring up at her with disbelieving eyes.

'Gina! It's really you! I thought you'd got fed up with visiting me. It's been simply ages.' The chair was propelled towards her and she bent to embrace and kiss its occupant.

'I'm sorry, Rusty darling. I should have written but, honestly, I thought I would have made it before this, especially as I'm living quite near here.'

'Living near here? Have you given up the flat? But that's marvellous!' the boy's freckled face lit up. 'Does that mean . . .'

'Perhaps living is a bit misleading. I should have said

working. But my job means living in, temporarily.' She pulled up a chair and sat close beside him, her arm about his shoulders.

'Aren't you running your agency any more?' Not even Rusty knew that Gina had taken over the role of Fantasy Woman and she doubted if he ever watched it any more. He would scarcely want to be reminded of the incident which had placed him in a hospital for spinal injuries.

'I still own the agency. But I'm working with a film company at the moment.' She hesitated, wondering whether she should tell him or not. But he would be bound to find out some time. 'Doing stunt work.'

As she had feared, his brown eyes clouded over and he ran his one good hand through the ginger hair that had given him his nickname.

'Oh no, Gina! I wish you wouldn't. Suppose something were to happen to you!'

'I'm very careful,' she promised him. 'We take every possible precaution.'

He grimaced. 'That's what they said about my ride with Mick and look what happened to us!'

'Miss Darcy?' A nurse was approaching down the ward. 'There's a gentleman asking for you. Is it all right if he comes in?'

'A gentle . . .?' Gina broke off as she recognised the tall, broad figure already striding purposefully in the nurse's wake. Tod Fallon! What was he doing here, she wondered resentfully? He must have followed her . . . again. Her cheeks began to burn angrily. Didn't he trust her out on her own? Her eyes narrowed. Or was it that he'd wanted to find out whom she was visiting? It was an unwarranted impertinence. It was no concern of his what she did with her free time.

'Do you intend to make a habit of following me?' she demanded irately, as soon as he was within earshot, but to her annoyance he totally ignored her remark, grinning in a friendly fashion at Rusty.

'Aren't you going to introduce me to your friend?'
There was a gleam of humour in Tod's dark eyes. Oh,
he could afford to look amused, now he knew her
'boyfriend' was a mere teenager. 'Or is he your
brother?' He looked from Gina's auburn head to
Rusty's ginger curls.

'Gosh!' Rusty exclaimed, 'I wish Gina were my sister.
Then I could live with her. She'd have me like a shot if
she could, but my sister can't be bothered. That's why I
have to stay here.'

'But you know you like it here, Rusty,' Gina
reminded him gently. 'They're very good to you and
you're improving a lot under their care. You'd be
awfully lonely in my flat all day, alone.' She turned to
Tod, grudgingly making the introduction he'd requested. 'This is Peter, known to his friends as Rusty,
for obvious reasons. Rusty, this is Mr Fallon, my
employer. He's a film director.'

'Gosh!' Peter was obviously impressed. 'I've heard of
you! You make super, exciting films. And Gina's
actually starring in one of your films?'

'Hold on!' Gina darted Tod a sour look as she
interrupted the enthusiastic boy. 'My face will never be
seen. I'm just a stand-in for the real star.'

'Oh?' Rusty asked interestedly. 'Someone famous?
Anyone I know?'

'No!' she said hastily.

'Mr Fallon?' Rusty looked up at Tod, his freckled
face drawn into lines of worry. 'Stunting is awfully
dangerous. You won't let anything happen to Gina, will
you?' Despite a manful effort, his lip quivered. 'She's all
the family I have now.'

'I thought you mentioned a sister?' Tod said gently.

The boy's face contorted with scorn.

'I don't count her. I don't care if I never see her
again. But Mr Fallon,' doggedly he repeated his
question, 'you won't let Gina get hurt?'

'I promise you, Rusty.' Tod squatted on his haunches, his right hand outstretched. 'As one man to another ... we'll take the greatest care of her. She's worth her weight in gold.'

Yes, Gina thought bitterly, as a fully trained stunter; not as a woman, not so far as Tod was concerned.

Rusty's face relaxed.

'Oh good! I'd hate to have *this* happen to her.' He indicated his wheelchair.

'What happened to you, old chap?'

'Can't we talk about something more cheerful?' Gina intervened hastily.

'I don't mind telling people about it,' Rusty assured her.

Rusty, as he preferred to be known, had in the early days of *Fantasy Woman* written in with a request and, since Fantasy Woman herself was an anonymous figure, the sponsors saw no reason not to humour her young relation's whim. For what Gina hoped the story now being told would not reveal was that Rusty's full name was Peter Durrant, that he was her cousin and Marcha's stepbrother.

Too young to drive, Peter had an urge to be a passenger in a fast car. It had been arranged for him to ride with a stuntman in a hair-raising chase scene. At the time, Gina, then only in an advisory capacity, had protested that it was far too dangerous, influenced also perhaps by the fact that her young step-cousin, unlike his sister, was a firm favourite of hers. But Rusty had been enthusiastically determined and Marcha had pooh-poohed her fears, all in favour of any scheme that would add panache to her programme. It didn't seem to matter to her that the life at risk was that of her young stepbrother.

It should have been a simple stunt, calling for the car to be driven towards five other oncoming vehicles and

weave between them. Originally the plan had been that
the car should travel at only thirty miles per hour and
the resulting film speeded up. But for some reason, the
film's director had decided that he wanted genuine
faster action.

When things had started to go wrong the television
camera crew had automatically gone on filming, but
Gina knew that they had been as horrified and shaken
as she by the subsequent tragedy. The speeding car,
narrowly missing the first approaching vehicle, hit the
next in an appalling smash-up. No one had ever found
out exactly what caused the accident, though ex-
amination of the wreck had suggested possible failure of
the steering system.

Rusty's retelling of the story resurrected the whole
picture: the fear; the stench of spilled petrol, of burning
rubber, of scorched and tortured metal; the chaos of
revolving lights as police cars, fire engines and
ambulances raced to the scene. Gina could hear quite
plainly the sound of grinding metal as the firemen had
cut away the buckled wreck, scarcely able to reach the
man and the boy inside.

Then there were doctors swarming over the vehicle,
giving painkillers, intravenous fluids; a pneumatic jack
had been shoved between doorpost and dashboard of
the wreck to wrench it apart. The mangled steering
wheel had been a horrible sight. The impact with it had
burst both of Mick's lungs; no wonder he hadn't
survived. Rusty, thank God, had, but he had been
badly injured, looked so vulnerable that Gina had
scarcely known how to restrain her tears. For Rusty's sake
she had controlled herself and, with her nursing training,
she had been able to give the medical team valuable
assistance. She had begged Marcha to stay and hold
Rusty's hand while the men worked, and later to go with
him in the ambulance, but Marcha had refused, running
in a blind panic from the scene of blood and carnage.

'Mick, the driver,' Rusty was telling Tod, 'was killed, and I ended up like this. Paraplegic they call it.'

'I know, son,' Tod said and Gina could see that he was genuinely moved by the story. He turned to Gina. 'And this happened on your programme? How *could* you permit such a . . .'

'It wasn't Gina's fault!' Rusty interrupted indignantly. 'She was the programme adviser and she didn't want me to do it. I can tell you, I wish I'd taken her advice. No, it was . . .'

'Rusty,' Gina interrupted, 'we must try not to blame anyone. It was an accident.'

The boy gave her a rueful grin.

'You're too charitable, Gina. I believe you'd defend the devil himself.' He went on with his story. 'The pain was awful. I thought I was dying. I wanted to die. But Gina was marvellous. She stayed with me the whole time, holding my hand. And she's been marvellous ever since. She's visited me whenever she can, once a fortnight usually. But it's been simply ages this time,' he concluded reproachfully, 'because of *you*.'

'I admit it, old man, it is my fault,' Tod apologised. 'I've kept Gina pretty busy these past weeks. But then I didn't know about you, you see. If I'd known she had a young friend in hospital, so near to my home, I'd have seen to it that she visited once a week at least, and from now on, I promise you, she will.'

Gina could see that Tod was now totally involved with Rusty's tragedy and she rather wished he wasn't, since further revelations could well prove awkward.

'Rusty,' she said gently, 'perhaps Mr Fallon and I ought to be going. We mustn't tire you.'

But the boy complained vigorously. 'When do I ever get tired?' he scoffed. 'You know you always stay for lunch and tea and take me out.'

'Tell you what,' Tod suggested before Gina could think of anything to say, 'if you and Gina don't mind me butting in, why don't we all go out somewhere together? My car is a big comfortable one. We could even drive out to my home, show you how a film is made.'

And Marcha would be there!

'No!' Gina said hastily, 'I don't think that would be a good idea. Too tiring for one day.'

'OK,' Tod said good-naturedly. 'Perhaps just a short spin then . . . and a pub lunch? Ever had a pub lunch, young man?'

Rusty was charmed and the outing was speedily arranged. But Gina was still on tenterhooks in case her young cousin should mention his relationship to Marcha. It was fortunate he didn't know his stepsister was involved in Tod's film. Though why Gina should feel any loyalty to Marcha . . . It just wasn't in her nature, she decided with a sigh, to be bitchy, to use her knowledge to discredit Marcha in Tod's eyes. After all, even if it did shock him enough to cause a breakdown in his relationship with Marcha, what did she, Gina, stand to gain? Precisely nothing.

Over lunch, Rusty was only too willing to give further details of his stay in hospital, of the months of agonising physical therapy.

'I think I'd have given up long ago and just become a vegetable if it hadn't been for Gina,' he confided. 'She told me I would improve gradually, if I worked at it. She said, "You've got to keep saying to yourself, one day I'll walk again, even if it takes years. I won't let the damned thing lick me". Though,' he looked slyly under his stubby eyelashes at Gina and her heart melted, '*she* said "bloody".'

'Extremely suitable,' Tod commented gravely.

Gina thought how very nice he could be when it suited him. Rusty needed a man to talk to sometimes, other than those on the hospital staff. He hadn't known his own father for very long.

'Gina was there the day when I first moved my right hand.' In between talking Rusty was demonstrating, very thoroughly, his ability to use it as he shovelled food into his mouth. 'I absolutely shrieked, didn't I, Gina? I said, "Did you see it? Did you see it?" And do you know what?' Rusty's voice was filled with puzzlement. 'She did the darnedest thing. She started to cry. Aren't women odd?'

'I've been convinced of that for a long time,' Tod concurred and for a brief instant his large hand came out and covered Gina's where it lay on the table, his eyes meeting hers in warm understanding.

'So I can write and eat. I hated being fed, like a great baby. I can even stand a bit now, on crutches. I'm going to walk one day, just like Gina said.'

Tod nodded emphatically. 'That you will!'

Gina was glad she and Tod must return home in separate cars. It meant she would not be subjected immediately to his cross-questioning. She was well aware that there were areas of Rusty's story which left room for speculation.

As the Mini, followed by the Rolls, swept into the parking area behind the house, Marcha appeared, moving at a brisker pace than was usual for her indolent nature. The older girl stood, impatiently tapping a foot, until both Tod and Gina had emerged from their respective vehicles.

'Where the hell have you been all day?' Her usual veneer of charm where Tod was concerned had slipped badly. 'Have you been with her?'

Gina didn't want to be involved in an emotional scene and she turned to go, but as she walked towards the rear entrance of the house she heard Tod say,

'Yes. We've been to Stoke Mandeville, to visit a very interesting and courageous young man.'

Oh Lord! Gina's stride faltered. That'd torn it. Now
Marcha would think . . . The tap of high heels pursuing
her over the uneven surface confirmed her conjecture.
Marcha's hand on her shoulder arrested her progress
and the older girl swung Gina round to face her.

Marcha's face was almost unrecognisable in its fury.
Careful of her blandly smooth complexion, she usually
avoided all strong expressions, the lines they brought in
their wake. Now the lovely features were contorted with
hatred . . . and fear.

'You took him to see Rusty? Why, for God's sake?'
she hissed. 'I suppose you've told him everything. I've
seen through you, Gina. You want Tod for yourself.
Don't think I can't recognise the signs, you . . . you
scheming little bitch. You stepped into my shoes once,
but only because I let you, because I didn't want the
rotten job any more. But you needn't think you're
going to repeat the performance here. This film is mine
and *Tod* is mine.'

'Marcha! For heaven's sake, calm down. I didn't tell
Tod anything. He knows about Rusty's accident, but
not who he is. Please don't credit me with having the
same underhand methods as you! If the positions had
been reversed, you'd have made damned sure Tod
heard all the sordid details.'

Marcha's face flushed an unbecoming brick red.

'OK,' she said grudgingly, 'so you didn't tell him. See
you don't, and keep him away from Rusty in future or
it's bound to come out. That little brat's always had it
in for me. I don't know why you bother with him. He's
only half related to us.'

'I bother with him because he's a nice kid, because
your stepmother was a nice woman, and, since she and
your father were killed, we're all the family Rusty's
got.'

'Count me out,' Marcha disclaimed. 'I don't want my
career hampered by having to tow a crippled brat

around with me. I never want to see him again and, remember, Tod's not to either.'

'He's not likely to,' Gina snapped, turning on her heel, unable to bear another second of her cousin's company, to listen to her unfeeling remarks.

But neither girl could control destiny, nor predict the actions of a man who was a law unto himself.

CHAPTER EIGHT

THERE seemed to be no logic in this film-making business. The story wasn't taken in chronological order. Later scenes were filmed before earlier ones and not until they were put together as a whole would it be possible to follow the plot in correct sequence.

So Gina discovered, when Tod told her they would now film the beginning of the story, at a point where hero and heroine were at odds, vying to outdo each other in their feats of daring, the heroine coming to grips with villainous men.

'I'll be needed then?' Gina asked.

'You certainly will!' Marcha told her, before Tod could answer. 'There's a lot of rough stuff involved and *I'm* not going to be slapped about,'—one slender hand caressed her own cheek—'I can't afford to have any bruises.' Gina was reminded of Marcha, in childhood, singing at a talent contest, 'My face is my fortune, sir, she said'. 'In fact,' Marcha concluded with an arch look at Tod which made Gina wince, 'apart from a couple of steamy love scenes, my work is finished.'

'Thinking of taking another holiday then?' the tall blonde Stephanie asked. 'Will it be Italy again? La Spezia, perhaps?'

'No!' Marcha snapped. 'And how many times do you need telling? It wasn't Italy. It was France . . . Nice.'

Gina had found herself a little disappointed in Tod lately. It was over a week since her visit to Rusty and, despite his promises, he hadn't once suggested that she take another day off to visit the boy. And when she had introduced the subject into conversation, he had adroitly changed its direction. He had seemed particularly remote and unapproachable for several days, not just to Gina, but to the whole of his workforce. The unit had seen very little of him; supervision of the shooting had been left to his assistant. Tod merely approved each day's rushes. Marcha had been showing distinct signs of petulance over his absences and Gina wondered if, like her, her cousin believed him to be seeing another woman, though Gina kept telling herself he would hardly neglect his work to do so.

But the early scenes he had mentioned required his presence. The script called for one of the gangsters to slap the heroine around, to actually connect with a punch, so that she was 'knocked out'. No wonder Marcha was only too pleased to let Gina do the scene. Tod, in his guise as the hero, would come to the heroine's rescue, defeating her opponent, assistance for which he would receive no thanks from the still prickly, independent heroine.

The scene was an indoor one, the confrontation taking place at the top of a wide sweeping, semicircle of stairs. After the blow, Gina must fall backwards and down the staircase.

'I don't envy you this one,' Stephanie told Gina, as they stood waiting for the action to commence. 'I've done something similar once or twice and the thought of it still scares me.'

'I must admit I don't feel too happy,' Gina confessed, 'but that's what I'm paid for!' She was aware of a smirking Marcha near at hand, waiting to see her fall, and she was determined not to let her cousin witness any reluctance on her part.

The fight scene went without a hitch, but just as the action reached the point where Gina must receive the knock-out blow, Tod called for a 'cut'.

Puzzled, Gina and her opposite number leant over the balustrade, watching, as Tod and his assistant went into a huddle. There seemed to be some disagreement

between them, but finally the assistant director spread
his hands in a gesture of defeat, nodded his head, then
took the stairs two at a time to where Gina stood.

'The boss isn't keen about you doing this stunt. He
says it's too risky for a novice. He's going to tell one of
the men to put on a wig and ...' He didn't get any
further with his explanation, as Gina brushed him
aside.

'Oh, no he's not!' she exploded. Her former
nervousness forgotten in indignation, she ran down the
stairs to where Tod stood, faced him, arms akimbo,
green eyes flashing. 'If you're not satisfied with my
work, at least have the decency to tell me so yourself.
I've practised for this and I'm going to do it.'

'Not if I say you don't.'

They stood, almost toe to toe, glaring at each other,
while an interested crew and cast waited for the
outcome of the duel. Knowing their boss, most of them
reckoned it was no contest. His word was law. He
might have a weakness for a pretty face, a seductive
body, but he was no woman's 'yes man'.

'You once accused me of cowardice,' Gina said, her
voice low but fierce.

'Oh! *That!*' Tod said wearily. 'God God, girl, don't
you know you've proved to me over and over again just
what you're made of. I know you have the courage of a
lioness, but you don't have to kill or maim yourself to
...' As he spoke, his firm tones wavered. 'Do you want
to end up like Rusty?' he demanded in a savage
undertone.

'No, of course not, but I've trained for this,' she
argued. 'Rusty hadn't, and besides, his injuries were an
accident.'

'Were they? Or were they the result of callous
indifference to safety measures?' There was a note of
challenging enquiry in his voice. 'The way I hear it, it
was the gross conceit and selfish unconcern of Fantasy

Woman that was responsible.' He watched her intently. What would her response be?

Gina was aware of the tension in him. It puzzled her. What was he expecting her to say? Just what had he learnt about that accident and from whom?'

'Who . . . who told you that?' she whispered. 'Rusty?' No, there'd been no opportunity.

'Marcha told me!' His tone was abrupt.

'Marcha?' Gina was taken aback. Was it possible she'd misjudged her cousin? Had Marcha found the moral fibre to confess her fault to Tod? Had they discussed Rusty during one of their intimate moments? Would they be bringing him to live at Mallions after they were married? If so, Gina should be rejoicing for the sake of the lovable teenager. But it wasn't joy that brought her heart sickeningly into her throat.

'Don't forget,' Tod was continuing, 'it was Marcha who told me her cousin was the famous Fantasy Woman when I suggested you as her double, because of your likeness to each other.'

'Marcha told you I was to blame?'

'Yes!' He was still watching her reactions closely.

'I see!' Cheeks flaming, eyes blazing, Gina hissed her retort at him. 'If that's what you believe, then there's all the more reason for me to perform this stunt. If it does go wrong and I do end up by crippling myself, it would only be justice in your eyes.' Before he could make any reply or further protest, she strode for the stairs, calling over her shoulder for the benefit of the waiting, wondering watchers. 'I'm not standing down for this stunt. I've worked for this and I'll damned well do it!'

'Right then!' Tod roared, his own temper obviously at flashpoint. 'Get on with it then, get it over, damn your eyes!'

God, but she was stubborn, he thought with reluctant admiration. His fingernails made deep impressions in the palms of his clenched hands. His anger with her stemmed from fear for her safety. He knew that. The possibility of Gina injured stirred primitive urges within him, even while he tried to tell himself he would feel equal concern for anyone performing so risky a stunt.

Gina mounted the stairs with every appearance of determination, hoping her legs didn't look as tremulous as they felt. It wasn't fear of the fall she was about to make that weakened her legs, but the awful despairing knowledge she had just gained. Tod didn't know Marcha had been Gina's predecessor in the role of Fantasy Woman. Marcha knew Gina too well, knew the younger girl would never stoop to defend herself by revealing Marcha's culpability. It was with almost a sense of fatalism that she launched herself into the fight scene once more.

As the contest moved towards its destined climax, Gina tried to think coolly and calmly of all the advice she had received during training. She must let herself go as fast as possible, yet remain relaxed and detached from the job. A pity, she thought wryly, that she couldn't approach her task in the boneless condition of intoxication. Falling drunks rarely harmed themselves.

The blow slammed home. It was a 'pulled' punch, but even so it carried enough impact to be painful. But there was no time to dwell on pain. She was falling, rolling, toppling. It was a horrible sensation, one to which she felt she would never become accustomed, never be able to approach with real sang-froid. But this was what she had wanted, worked for: personal involvement, even though she would still remain an anonymous figure. There would be no star billing for her, not even a credit. Everyone, except a few professionals, seeing the finished product would think Marcha had done all her own stuntwork, as Mary Pickford and Helen Gibson had done in the early days of filming.

'Gina?' Tod was bending over her, holding out a

hand to pull her to her feet. 'You OK?' And, as she nodded rather shakily, 'Sure? If you're in any doubt, any pain whatsoever, we'll have the doc check you over right away.'

Tod always made a point of having a doctor present during the filming of dangerous scenes and his concern, she reminded herself, would have been just as great for any other member of his team.

'Surely you're not satisfied with *that* take?' Marcha drawled. 'I thought it an extremely clumsy effort. It ought to be done again.' For heaven's sake! Did Marcha want her to break her neck, Gina wondered groggily! 'After all,' her cousin was continuing, 'it is my image that's at stake.'

Gina was not the only one taken aback by the sudden savage fury in Tod's face and voice as he turned on Marcha.

'I'm totally satisfied!' he snapped. 'Gina knows her job. You should consider yourself fortunate I didn't insist on you doing your own stuntwork.'

The stunned expression on Marcha's face should have been funny, and indeed there was no doubt that the film crew found it so. Marcha was not popular and there were subdued and not so subdued titters of laughter, at which Marcha flounced angrily away to the edge of the crowd. But Gina knew the incident had only increased Marcha's enmity towards her; while the cousins had never been friends, at least until Tod had brought them together there had existed an unarmed hostility, an unspoken agreement to differ.

The fight sequence completed, Gina's work on the film was finished. Over the preceding weeks she hadn't wanted to look ahead to the end of this period in her life. While it had not been exactly happy, her emotions were too torn for that, it had been eventful, stimulating. She had enjoyed knowing and being known by a large group of people. To her surprise, she found she had no desire to return to the peaceful isolation of her flat and now she realised that she had no idea what was to happen next. Would she be retained for further stuntwork, or was this it, a one-off? Was she expected to leave now, go back to television? Unfortunately, in view of her reluctance to confront Tod, there was only one way to find out: to ask him. And that involved choosing just the right moment since she didn't want to raise the subject before the rest of the team. But on the other hand she was reluctant to seek Tod out on his own.

In the event, the decision of when to tackle him was taken out of her hands by Tod himself.

That same evening she had been sitting with Melanie again, while Sally kept what had now become a regular date with one of the cameramen. Much of Gina's time had been spent in brooding on the uncertainty of her future, even more on the hopelessness of her love for Tod. Feeling somewhat depressed, she emerged from the nursery suite to find him waiting for her.

'After the day you've had, you shouldn't be sitting up so late,' he growled, taking her arm in a fierce grip, which, while it hurt, sent a thrill of ecstasy, far more agonising, darting throughout her entire being.

'There'll be plenty of time for rest, now the film's over,' Gina told him. But her voice was shaky and she felt stupid tears blur her eyes. She wished she did not have to encounter Tod right now. It was fatigue of course. In the morning she would be better able to face the knowledge that the time had come for her to leave Mallions. She wasn't needed here any more, not in any capacity.

Tod was drawing her along a passageway into a wing of the house she had not yet seen, but which she knew housed his private quarters.

'That's what I want us to talk about,' he told her.

'Your future plans. We may as well discuss them in comfort, over a drink.'

A heavy door opened into a sitting-room, whose occupancy was so obviously male that it seemed an extension of Tod's personality. Comfortable, but purely functional, it had none of the little personal touches a woman would have added. If there had been any reminders that once Maria had shared these rooms, they had been removed.

'Do they really concern you?' Gina asked wearily as she refused the drink. 'I thought my agreement with you was only for the duration of this film. If your "star" needs a double in your next production, count me out.'

'You're contracted to TLM Enterprises,' he reminded her, as he indicated by gesture that she should be seated, 'and, technically, I now *am* TLM Enterprises.'

Which was clear enough for anyone to understand. She was bound to him. Of course she could ask to be released from her contract. She told him so.

His answering smile was hawkish, making her uneasy, an unease which proved to be valid.

'You should have read the small print more closely. Our agreement binds you to me for three years and, while I *could* release you if I felt so inclined, I must warn you, I don't intend to do so.'

'I could break the contract, just walk out!' she said, a touch of her normal spirit in her tone.

'In which case I could sue you. But if you prove difficult, there's a much easier way. Remember the security precautions? They can keep people in as well as out.'

She stared at him, green eyes wide with disbelief. This was pure melodrama.

'You mean you'd actually go so far as to . . . to . . .'

'Yes,' he said simply.

She was still near to tears. He couldn't do it, could he? It was illegal, immoral. She was entitled to *personal*

freedom even if she were tightly bound by her contract
to work for him. And what about her visits to Rusty?
Suppose she were immured here indefinitely, unable to
see him, the boy would think she, too, had abandoned
him.

'That's . . . that's . . .'

'Blackmail,' Tod said unexpectedly. She wouldn't
have expected him to admit it. 'You see, Gina . . .' He
joined her on the settee, placing himself so close to her
that they touched at shoulder, hip and thigh, and the
heat his body exuded seemed to penetrate the very
fabric of the wrap she wore. 'You see, I don't intend to
let you just walk out of my life. It would be impossible,
now.' He reached out for her and, as he pulled her into
his arms, she felt a weakening warmth engulf her body.
Her eyes seemed unable to drag their mesmerised gaze
from that attractive mouth now smiling crookedly at
her. 'We have to try and work something out.' His
voice was throaty and she recognised the fire of passion
that leapt dangerously in his dark eyes.

'Tod . . . I . . .' She licked painfully dry lips. 'You
can't *enjoy* keeping someone against their will . . .'

'No,' he agreed. 'I'd far rather you stayed willingly.
Will you stay, Gina?'

'No,' she croaked, 'I can't . . . I . . .'

'You're afraid,' he accused, 'afraid to admit the truth,
that you *want* to stay. You still want me, Gina. Oh,
you've tried to pretend. You even tried to make me
think you were interested in Gibson, but I soon saw
through that. Why do you have to be so damnably
proud? Why not admit what your body tells me?'

If it were *only* her body, Gina thought miserably,
perhaps she could bring herself to have a casual affair
with him. But heart and mind were too closely involved
with what her body felt, and all three would be broken
on the wheel of despair if she gave herself to him on his
terms.

'Please let me go,' she whispered. 'You . . . you said we'd come here to talk business.'

'I brought you here,' Tod said, his voice raw with undisguised emotion, 'because I wanted to make love to you. Because I'm going to make love to you.'

'No! No, damn you! Oh, why can't you be satisfied with Marcha?' It was a cry of despair. 'Or does it turn you on because I'm so like her? Well, we're not alike, not under the surface.'

'No, you most certainly are not,' he agreed obscurely. 'This has nothing to do with Marcha. *This* is you, Gina, you and me.'

She had taken a bath earlier, to ease some of the bruises gained during filming, and, since she was only going to sit with Melanie, she hadn't bothered to dress again, slipping along to the child's rooms in nightdress and robe. She had never expected to encounter Tod, believing him to be out as usual, with Marcha, or at whatever mysterious rendezvous he'd been keeping of late.

Now his hands were dexterously parting the front edges of her dressing-gown, had it open before she could prevent him. In fact, one hand trapped both of hers, while with his free one he continued to reveal the warm, curvaceous swell of her breasts, their contours outlined by the soft, smooth silk crossover front of her nightdress.

Common sense, pride, told her she should repulse him; use feet and legs, since her hands were captive; but her body seemed independent of her brain, her breasts hardening against the soft fabric, a shudder of fierce, breathtaking pleasure destroying all will-power as his dark head bent and his mouth pushed aside the flimsy barriers, until he found the scented shadowy cleft between her breasts.

'Tod! Please! Don't!' Mingled pain and pleasure drew the tortured plea from her. But it was only a token

protest and they both knew it, for he freed her hands
which had ceased to struggle in his clasp, his whole
attention centred now on holding, cupping her breasts,
while his tongue wrote moist, burning messages of
desire against the creamy flesh, igniting a thousand
aching, answering fires within her.

As her arms went about his neck, he gathered her up
and rose, all in one easy movement, carrying her
towards a door which led into an adjoining bedroom.

Her heart was drumming so loudly, it deafened her to
the words he was muttering against her throat, her
temples, her mouth. He dealt swiftly, competently, with
the removal of her dressing-gown and nightdress, before
setting her down in the centre of his bed. She was past
all protesting now, with no time to be shy or
embarrassed by her nakedness. He knelt over her, his
mouth moving lingeringly over her from throat to
breast, down over her ribcage, the silken smoothness of
her stomach, his tongue making sudden erotic,
tormenting little forays that left her gasping, half
senseless with the urgent need for fulfilment.

Tod knew there was no need for tentativeness on his
part as if Gina had been an untutored virgin, but made
an assured, sensuous progression towards what he knew
they both desired. She was already a woman, a woman
starved, ripe and hungry to know a man's possession
once more, but above all, *his* possession. Despite all her
dissembling, to an experienced man all the signs were
there, plainly to be seen. He wanted her, wanted her
more than he had ever desired any other woman, since
Maria; and he realised with a sense of wonder that the
pain of that loss had become less in these last few
weeks, knew that the miracle had been achieved by the
presence of Gina in his life, in his home. It wasn't, as
Gina had accused him, because of her superficial
resemblance to Marcha. Since he had met Gina, seeing
her, knowing her, was like possessing the print of a

photograph after having only seen the negative. He knew she had penetrated the armour he had grown slowly and painfully during the years since Maria.

Gina's fingers fumbled frantically with the buttons of his shirt, with the waistband of his trousers.

'Help me, please help me.' She muttered the words against the slightly rough texture of his jaw and throat, a sensual stimulus that increased the intensity of the sensations riding her.

Together they removed his shirt, sliding it from his muscular body, the roughness of his chest hair brushing her breasts in erotic tantalisation. Desperately she whispered his name, her hands spanning his back, her gripping fingers raising weals on his naked flesh, causing him to cry out in husky pleasure as his mouth covered hers, his tongue plunging again and again in simulated possession.

'Tod, love me . . . oh, love me!' Her whispered plea was almost lost against the warm, sweat-bedewed dampness of his shoulder.

'I will . . . I do . . .' came his fervent reply.

Somehow he had discarded his trousers and now, as he lowered himself against her, the hirsute flatness of his stomach, the thrust of his desire against her, the acute sensation, brought a sobbing breath from her throat.

His hands shaped her hips, curved around beneath her, lifting her towards him. In the light that filtered through from the room beyond, she could just make out his features, knew he was watching her face, waiting for her reaction.

'Was it ever like this with your husband?' he demanded suddenly, the words accompanied by an increasing pressure of his body upon hers that forbade her to answer in the affirmative. He need not have feared. There was no comparison. She had never loved before, not like this.

'No . . .' She could scarcely speak. Speech was the last thing she wanted of him now; all she wanted was for him to fill this empty, aching cavern within her.

'Tonight I'm going to make you forget there ever was another man in your life,' he promised huskily.

Molten heat built between her thighs, her body craved that final union and she moved against him, an involuntary convulsion of fluttering nerves. Then there was no more delay, only a series of movements, mounting in their intensity. Again her hands contoured his back, traced his spine, caressed the sensitive spot at its base, feeling the unmistakable shudder of response that ran through him. She felt those shudders grow in intensity as she arched into him.

'I've wanted this for so long,' he groaned huskily, 'wanted you for so long.'

Desperately she pressed kisses against his jaw, the corner of his mouth, the closed lids of his eyes. It was heaven to feel and taste the salty flavour of his male body, to know the increasing intimacy with it. She didn't know how much longer she could bear this feverish insanity of longing. Then, as though in answer to her unspoken cry for mercy, he was between her thighs, his arms locking her to him as he moved into the rhythm of possession.

Something seemed to snap within her, all the months of pent-up emotions, of self-denial, the belief that love was not for her ever again, and she cried out her satisfaction at the same moment that Tod uttered her name; it was a sound of awed jubilation.

For a moment or two there was nothing but sweet release, the aftermath of lethargy. Then she began to realise what she had done. Despite all her vows to the contrary, she had become one of Tod's women. What she had felt for him had been love, a need to give of that love, freely, generously; but in spite of that there had been no sign, no indication from him, other than that of physcial need.

In a sudden access of self-loathing, she wrenched herself away from the heavy encircling arm, the hand that still covered one love-swollen breast.

'Gina? What is it? What's wrong?' Instantly his senses were alert and he half raised himself to look at her.

'You know what's wrong, damn you!' she whispered, as she scrabbled on the floor, looking for her robe. 'Damn you for . . . for making me . . .'

'For making you want me?' he challenged softly. His eyes, warm with remembered satisfaction, were also gently laughing at her. 'I didn't have to do anything about that. You've wanted me for a long time, Gina. All I did was to help you cast aside your inhibitions, make you admit it.'

'And what good has that done me?' she demanded as she dragged the belt of her robe, jerking it in a tight, double knot, a belated precaution. 'It seems to me you're the one who's benefited, by a build-up to your already inflated ego, by having your sexual appetite appeased. Did you have to have me as well as Marcha?'

'No!' he said softly, eyes and voice caressing her. 'Instead of!'

'Instead . . .' She gasped, then broke off, speculation rife within her. Marcha, it seemed, had fallen into the same trap as her predecessors; she had begun to be too possessive and Tod was retreating to his defensive position; and what better defence than to install another woman in Marcha's place? Only Gina wasn't going to be used like that. 'Sorry Tod,' she said, trying to steady her voice as she retreated towards the door. 'But you'll have to look elsewhere for your substitute. Tonight was . . . was . . .'

'A glorious experience for both of us, and you know it.' The sensuousness in his voice sent shudders racing along her spine.

'I was going to say it was a mistake,' she continued more firmly. 'You took an unfair advantage, caught me tired and off guard. But it won't happen again.'

He made no move, but his voice was husky, mocking as he said,

'Oh, yes it will, Gina. You'll see. Now that you know how it can be between us, you'll crave it, like a drug, every time we're together.'

And, God help her, she knew he was right; that was why they mustn't be together again. She must get away. She must!

'I'll find some way of getting out of here,' she told him defiantly. 'Some way out of that contract. This is the twentieth century. There's no way you can hold me prisoner indefinitely.'

'No?' The amusement, the arrogant self-confidence in his voice made her uneasy. 'I wasn't going to tell you this. It could have been against my own interests, but not now, I think. The only way you could be released from that contract is if you were to become pregnant. Obviously a stuntwoman in that condition would be very little use.'

She stared at him. Oh, the irony of it.

'On the other hand . . .' His eyes roved over her in a considering way that brought an involuntary, convulsive flutter to her stomach muscles. 'Pregnancy could keep you here just as effectively. Either way I win. Wouldn't you agree?' Then, before she could answer, 'I'd like a son.'

'That's something you'll have to ... to apply to Marcha for.' She nearly choked on the words. If he had been deliberately seeking for some way in which to hurt her he couldn't have succeeded better. If he only knew it, she would like nothing better than to give him the son he wanted. It might bind him to her and it would mean as much to her in other ways, but it just wasn't possible.

'Marcha?' Unaware of her mounting distress, he was smiling broadly. 'Marcha is a career woman. She wouldn't dream of risking her future . . . or her figure.'

'Not even for the chance of marrying you?' she couldn't help asking and felt the immediate rejection in him.

'I've no intention of marrying Marcha,' he said coldly.

'Or anyone else?' she returned shrewdly, and felt a chill within herself as he dipped his dark head in agreement.

'But Gina . . .' he began, holding out his hand to her.

'No!' She didn't let him finish. Dared not. Every nerve in her body was still highly sensitised. Now that she had known intimacy with him, she knew that if he attempted a repetition of his lovemaking she would succumb just as easily. 'You've said enough, Tod. I get the picture, quite clearly . . . and I want you to know this. I despise you. Oh yes . . .' as he seemed about to protest, 'I despise you . . . But I despise myself just as much. When my marriage broke up, I swore I'd never risk getting involved with another man, that I'd never marry again. So in a way I can understand how you felt about Maria. Marriage is an entanglement, it's an inextricable relationship painful to get out of, to forget. Just for a while there, you made me forget my resolution and I'm bitterly ashamed of myself. Sex without love, without commitment, is just lust and we've just been guilty of one of the deadliest sins.'

'Gina, wait a moment. I . . .'

'No!' she said again. She backed towards the door. 'You may think you've got the upper hand. But I'll break that contract somehow. I won't stay here, give you a chance to catch me off guard again . . .'

'And if you become pregnant?' His words were cut off as she began to laugh, wildly, hysterically.

'Even *you* aren't man enough for that!' she cried, despair in her voice.

'Why! You little . . .'

'Oh, don't worry! Much as I'd like to dent your intolerable ego, I don't stoop to insults of that kind. What you don't realise . . . what I've never told anyone else . . .' she was sobbing jerkily now, 'is that I can't get pregnant . . . not by you . . . or any other man. I'm barren. Do you hear me, barren. I'm no use to anyone . . . not even to myself . . . and certainly no use to you! Look elsewhere for your son . . .'

With these words she fled and, such was the shock she'd dealt him, his reactions were delayed long enough for her to reach her own room, to lock its door against intrusion.

CHAPTER NINE

AFTER not expecting to sleep at all, Gina overslept. Groggily, she supported herself on one elbow in order to look at the bedside clock she'd forgotten to set, wondering what *had* finally woken her.

The sound of voices raised in altercation drifted up from the courtyard below. Wide awake now, for surely one of those voices didn't belong here, she ran to the window, threw it open and leant out. A curious little tableau was being enacted.

Tod's car stood, doors still wide open. In his wheelchair, beside the car, sat Rusty, Tod's hand on his shoulder as, together, they faced Marcha's spitting venom.

'So this is what it's all about. This crippled brat! A fine pack of lies I dare say he's told you ... he and Gina between them.'

'Don't you dare say anything against Gina, you bitch!' Rusty began, but Tod silenced him.

'No, Rusty! She's not worth your breath. Gina,' he continued harshly, not shouting, but overriding Marcha's frustrated mewls of rage, 'Gina has more decency and loyalty in her little finger than you possess in your whole body. She hasn't a malicious bone in her. What I've learnt about you, Marcha, has been from other sources, merely confirmed by Rusty here. I wondered how anyone could be so callous as to subject a boy of Rusty's age to such a dangerous risk and, in spite of what you told me, I couldn't reconcile that kind of behaviour with what I've learnt of Gina's character.'

'It was at Rusty's own insistence.' Marcha managed to insert the excuse.

'Maybe! But as his next-of-kin you had the power to veto it. Gina begged that it shouldn't be allowed, but you welcomed the risk, didn't you?' His tone became contemptuous. 'As far as you were concerned it was one well worth taking, and not just for the sake of your programme ratings. Only it didn't quite come off, did it?'

'I don't know what you mean.' Marcha was trembling visibly now, not with rage, but with what seemed to the watching Gina to be an ague of fear.

'Piecing together what Rusty's told me, plus information from your late father's solicitor ... that your father left everything to your stepbrother ... it seems to me Rusty's death would have been very convenient for you. No wonder you couldn't wait to get away from the scene of the accident. Even you, my dear Marcha, weren't hard boiled enough to witness the outcome of your "calculated" risk. I wonder what it felt like, for those few hours until they told you Rusty would live, to feel like a murderess?'

'This is all rubbish, guesswork,' Marcha cried shrilly. 'How could I know there would be such a dreadful accident? You can't prove a thing like that.'

'No,' Tod agreed, 'you couldn't know, but you could hope ... And no, I haven't any proof, luckily for you. But I'm certain enough in my own mind. Get out of my house, Marcha! You've got an hour.'

'I've also got a contract,' she cried triumphantly. 'I still have two more films to do. I could sue you.'

'Go ahead! It would be worth the money to be rid of you. But I don't think you'll succeed. In fact I don't think you'll even try, just in case I let a few rumours leak out.'

Breathlessly, Gina waited for her cousin's reaction. Would it be one of further defiance? But it seemed the older girl realised she had lost. Yet she retained sufficient of her normal hauteur to enquire,

'I presume I'm allowed to use the telephone to make my arrangements?'

'Obviously you'll need to call a taxi,' Tod said, 'since I've no intention of chauffeuring you anywhere.'

Gina felt like cheering as Marcha turned away and flounced out of sight, back into the house, but her main concern now was with showering, getting dressed and going downstairs to see Rusty. It was obvious what he was doing here. Tod had brought the boy to confront his stepsister, so Marcha could be in no doubt that Tod possessed all the facts he claimed. But how long had Tod known that Rusty was Marcha's stepbrother?

En route to search for her young cousin, Gina heard Marcha using the library telephone.

'OK.' Her voice sounded angry, sulky. 'So the moment's finally come. Yes, today! I've only got an hour.' Obviously she was making use of her access to the telephone to call friends, as well as the necessary taxi. It seemed she had been expecting her cards sooner or later, and yet, only a few weeks ago, Marcha had seemed so positive she would be marrying Tod. At any rate it had seemed certain that she would retain her position as '*maîtresse en titre*'.

'Hallo, Rusty darling!' She had tracked them down to the breakfast room, where morning coffee was being served. There was a host of other people milling about, for which Gina was relieved. There would be no opportunity for Tod to approach her, to give the conversation a personal turn; and, by the time the last of the film crew had filtered away, she would have done likewise, for she had made her plans, knew how she was going to escape.

'Gina! Gosh, am I glad to see you. I've got so much to tell you, you wouldn't believe.' The words fairly cascaded out of the excited boy and Gina tried to look suitably surprised as he related the conversation, most of which she'd already overheard. 'And Tod says I'm to *live* here . . . actually live *here*, as if it was my real home, and only go to the hospital for my treatment. He's a great guy, Gina!' Rusty gazed with admiring eyes at Tod as he stood talking to one of his crew.

As if she didn't know that, Gina thought miserably. In her eyes he was damned near perfect, except for one thing, his reluctance to marry again. Yet, in fairness, she couldn't blame him for an aversion she'd once held herself.

'He's been to visit me almost every day since that first time. We've been making all kinds of plans, you can't imagine. And he says you'll be staying here, too, Gina. Is that right?'

'No,' she said curtly, then, at the boy's surprised look, softened her tone, 'I'm afraid that's impossible. You know how busy I am . . . and the flat's my home.'

Rusty's freckled face was downcast, but not for long.

'Oh, well,' he said cheerfully, 'I guess he must have got it wrong. But I dare say you'll still come and visit me?'

'Oh . . . I . . .' But before she could think of a suitably non-committal reply which would satisfy the boy, there was a general interruption.

Sally rushed into the room, face and figure both expressive of agitation.

'Oh, Mr Fallon! Thank goodness I've found you all together. Now you'll all be able to look for her.'

'Look for whom?' Tod asked sharply. 'You don't mean . . .'

'Yes! Melanie! I can't find her anywhere.'

'When did you last see her?'

'About half an hour ago. We discovered her kitten was missing. She was so upset. I . . . I told her to stay in her room while I looked for him. But this is such a big house and he's such a tiny thing. I didn't realise I'd been gone so long and . . . and when I got back to the nursery, Melanie wasn't there.'

'Did it never occur to you that she's probably hunting for the damned thing herself? I *knew* the dratted animal would cause trouble of some sort.' An indignant Gina received the full force of his irritated scowl. 'We'll soon find her, Sally. Don't worry. Some of us will search the house and others the garden.'

This was her chance, Gina thought. Every inclination told her she, too, ought to join in the search for Melanie but, as Tod had said, it shouldn't prove a long one and for once she was going to put herself first.

'I'll try the garden,' she murmured and, in the general hubbub of noise and movement, she slipped out of the house.

Moving slowly at first, pretending to look about her, she finally reached the trees, then began to run, only emerging from cover when she reached the edge of the airstrip. Sliding back the door, she entered the hangar. Would the Cessna have enough fuel for her to reach a suitable place to land, far enough from Tod's clutches? She scrambled into the cockpit, flicked switches and anxiously inspected dials. She drew a breath of relief. The tanks were full.

Just to think, flying had once been a source of terror to her and now it was to prove a means of salvation. She taxied out on to the runway and was soon airborne. She had no idea where she was headed. Her main preoccupation had been to take off before Tod got wind of her plan and prevented it.

Her flight path took her over the house and the main gate and she was just heaving a wistful little sigh of nostalgia, when something strange arrested her attention. The large iron gates which, when shut, completed the circuitry of electronic warning devices, were standing open, unattended.

Forgetting her former urgency, Gina circled. Her curiosity was rewarded as two figures emerged from the gatehouse, a woman and a child ... Marcha and Melanie!

Gina's first thought was that Marcha had magnanimously postponed her departure, put aside her own feelings to help search for the missing child. But this conjecture didn't stand up to inspection. Marcha didn't like children; she wasn't the sort to forgive and forget a slight, much less a direct attack upon herself and the discovery of her past action. And Tod had made it pretty clear what he thought of her perfidy towards Rusty. No, Marcha might be said to have a score to settle.

She'd had nearly an hour in which to carry out her revenge and fate seemed to have played into her hands with the missing kitten. Or ... Gina didn't believe in coincidence ... had Marcha contrived that disappearance?

Living and working here, the older girl would obviously know about the gatehouse control system. She would know, as Gina did, that Andy and Greg were bound to join in searching house and immediate grounds. Nothing easier than for her to reach the control point unobserved. But how had she persuaded Melanie to accompany her, when their dislike was mutual? Of course! Simple! She had only to pretend she'd seen the kitten wandering down the drive!

But, puzzled Gina as she circled again, how did Marcha intend to proceed from here? It would be pointless to just walk out. Once the break in security was discovered, it would be no time at all before Marcha was overtaken, particularly as she would be hampered by the slower speed of the child. The taxi! Marcha's telephone call!

Marcha was standing by the gates, obviously waiting, one hand restraining Melanie, who appeared to be struggling. Then two things happened simultaneously. A large limousine raced up the road, halting in the gateway long enough to bundle woman and child into the interior. Then it proceeded *onwards, into the grounds of Mallions!* That was no taxi!

The second occurrence gave Gina the clue to this apparently strange proceeding. To her right, and slightly above her, appeared a helicopter. There was every indication that it was descending towards the airstrip, from which she herself had taken off only minutes before.

Gina's swift thought processes had made her the successful businesswoman she was. Within an instant of recognising the intruder's intentions, surmising that this was another attempt by the Mantalinis, aided and abetted by Marcha, she was heading the Cessna back towards base, faster than the helicopter could travel.

The black limousine had reached the airstrip and was stationary, its occupants waiting for the helicopter to land. No use Gina setting down. She hardly imagined herself to be a match for the men in it. It was as the helicopter neared the ground that she realised what she must do. She must stop anyone leaving the car, she must undertake the most dangerous stunt of her career to date, low-level flying. But she didn't think twice about it.

Down she plummeted, then she began to fly backwards and forwards over the car, dipping first one wing then another, keeping between car and helicopter. She wasn't unduly surprised to hear the crack of bullets, to learn that the would-be kidnappers were armed. A bullet hit and ricocheted off the bodywork of the Cessna and she was thankful it hadn't struck the cockpit window. After several runs, she was beginning to wonder how much longer she could continue before a bullet found its target . . . her.

But help was at hand. Two or three cars were now streaming towards the airstrip: Tod's and those she recognised as belonging to Greg and Andy. The breach in their defences had been discovered. She made one more overhead pass and then, the pilot obviously opting for discretion rather than valour, the helicopter took off. Without its support, the occupants of the car seemed to decide it was futile to continue and, as Gina circled again, gaining height, she was relieved to see Marcha and Melanie pushed from the car, which then took off at great speed.

Greg and Andy drove in pursuit, but Tod was out of his car, running to where his daughter was just scrambling up from the grass. Gina waited only long enough to see that the child was safe, then she turned the aircraft away, not seeing Tod's frantic signals, flying blind for a moment or two as tears stung her eyes, tears at the memory of Tod with Melanie in his arms. Did he even realise who had played such a large part in his daughter's rescue? Did he care?

'Well Miss . . . Mrs? . . . Ah, Miss Darcy, I don't know if this is good news or bad.'

Gina sat on the edge of her seat, hands tightly clasped. Her throat worked convulsively as she awaited the verdict.

'It's quite conclusive. You are pregnant! Oh dear! Oh dear, dear!' The doctor's homely features contorted into lines of distress as Gina burst into tears. She rounded her desk, proffering a box of tissues, a glass of water, kindly platitudes.

'H-how is it possible?' Gina gulped after a while, after she had told the other woman of her utter delight, that her tears were those of happiness. 'Th-they told me I'd never get pregnant again, never.'

Doctors had been wrong before, this sympathetic one told her. Sometimes things changed, righted themselves. There were so many imponderables in the human physiology. 'But I don't think we need trouble ourselves with all that, do you? The next obvious step is to provide for your welfare and the baby's. Is yours a professional name, my dear? Are you married?'

'No, I'm not married and the father isn't going to know anything about it. This baby is going to be mine . . . just mine.'

If Tod ever found out, he would surely claim it, particularly if it turned out to be a boy.

It was just six weeks since Gina had flown away from Mallions and had been fortunate enough to secure permission to land on another private strip. She'd been uncertain at first whether it was safe to return to her flat, or whether she should move out, covering her tracks. But with Tod's resources it was unlikely she could evade him forever, so she might as well save herself the trouble. In the event, he had made no attempt to contact her and gradually she relaxed. He wasn't going to follow up his seduction of her. She ought to feel relief, and in one sense she did, but it was mingled with pique that his attraction towards her should have been so transitory, his pursuit of her so easily abandoned. But worse than the pique was the ache in her heart, in her body. How long did it take for such pains to ease?

Two weeks ago, certain symptoms which, taken in conjunction with other facts, had added up to a suspicion, an unlikely circumstance, which at first she had discarded as being totally impossible. But the signs had persisted and she had decided to consult a gynaecologist.

She hadn't worked since she'd returned to London. There had been no point in contacting TLM Enterprises, since Tod held sway there. But now, though she was by no means impoverished, she knew she must think of her baby's future. The GD Agency was still running profitably and, rather than just sit back and receive the proceeds, Gina decided she would return there, take up the reins once more herself. With a brief break for her child to be born, she would be fully occupied, with no time to brood about Tod Fallon, to wonder whom he had found to fill Marcha's place, the place he had invited her, Gina, to take.

'Hallo? Gina Darcy speaking!'

She had heard the telephone's insistent ring as she'd stepped out of the lift and inserted her key in the front door of the flat.

'Oh, Miss Darcy, thank goodness!' It was her secretary. 'Just after you left the office, we had a client call in. He said he had a most urgent request to make and he insisted he would only speak to you.'

Gina sighed wearily. It had been a long day and she was tired and hungry. She seemed to have less stamina these days.

'Did you get his number? I'll ring him.'

There was a slight hesitation at the other end, as if the girl expected a reprimand for what she was about to say.

'He . . . he wouldn't give me a telephone number. He said he wanted to speak to you, face to face.'

'You didn't give him my address?' Gina snapped out the question. Her staff had strict instructions, but this girl was new.

'He . . . he said he knew where you lived, that he'd call round. I said I'd telephone you, warn you to expect him, but he said I wasn't to. He . . . he was quite fierce. I was worried. Miss Darcy, do you want me to call the police? . . . Miss Darcy? . . . *Miss Darcy*?'

'Yes? Oh, sorry! No, Babs, I don't think that will be necessary. But you did right to warn me. Thanks.'

What had begun as an irritating interruption to her free time had, while the secretary spoke, assumed a more menacing aspect. It was Tod. It had to be. Only he and Jimmy Riley knew her home address and Jimmy wasn't aware that she was back in London.

Thanks to her secretary she had a few precious moments in which to decide her course of action. She could pretend to be out or she could make it an actuality: leave her flat and spend the evening elsewhere. But why should she run away, be driven out of her own home? And any evasive action she took would only give her a temporary reprieve.

Tod, as she had cause to remember, could be very persistent. Better to get the encounter over, make it quite clear that she never wanted to see him again. It wasn't true of course. Underlying her determination to outface him was a nagging curiosity to know the purpose of his visit and, even stronger, an insidious longing to see him.

The doorbell rang and her heart skipped a beat. He was here and she hadn't even had time to do anything about her appearance. She was still wearing the smart, but rather severe grey dress she affected for office work. Her make-up was probably non-existent and her hair! She groaned. She had meant to wash it tonight.

What did any of that matter? she asked herself sternly, as she went to answer the bell's now more insistent summons. But she couldn't resist a swift assessment of herself in the hall's full length mirror. Anxiously, she ran her hands over her hips, the slight curve of her belly. She didn't think her condition showed yet.

The ringing had ceased and now her caller was raining blows on the front door.

'Gina! Open up! I know you're in there, damn you!'

She flung the door open, surprising him with his fists still raised.

'For heaven's sake. Do you want all the neighbours to hear?'

'In this place?' he scoffed, inserting himself into the hallway so adroitly she couldn't have prevented him from doing so even if that had been her intention. 'I bet it's so well soundproofed you could commit murder without being overheard.'

She turned around, leaving him to shut the door, and preceded him into the living area. It was taking every ounce of her determination to appear cool and poised when, inwardly, she was a mass of nervous speculation. She seated herself on a chair so that, if he wanted to sit down, he would be forced to place himself some distance from her. The only trouble was he showed no inclination to settle anywhere, roaming to and fro restlessly.

Gina was determined she wouldn't be the first to open the subject of his visit. She sat quietly, hands folded, eyes steady, giving a deceptive impression of cold disinterest.

Hell's bells! Tod thought, shooting a glance at her from beneath lowering brows. Why did she have to make it so difficult for him to begin? Why didn't she say something, ask why he was here, even get mad at him, so that he had an excuse to take hold of her, an action which had obsessed him mentally and physically for some considerable time? She was even lovelier than he remembered. Despite her obvious end-of-day fatigue, there was some indefinable luminous quality about her, an added serenity which he longed to disturb.

'Aren't you going to ask me why I'm here?' He shot the question at her suddenly, abruptly, when the silence had become too strained to endure.

'No, since I've no doubt you'll enlighten me eventually.' Her tone was maddeningly remote and Tod took a grip of himself. He must match her coolness. With this intention, he threw himself down in the sunken lounging area and looked up at her, his view a distorted one, beginning with her primly folded legs, long and shapely in sheer nylon. He swallowed, averted his eyes.

'I want to thank you for what you did, for your part in rescuing Melanie.'

'A letter would have done,' she told him quietly.

Confound it. He couldn't sit down here, at a disadvantage. He got up and came to stand over her.

'A letter would *not* have done! You took a considerable risk, flying so low. The least I could do was to thank you personally.'

'It took you long enough,' she observed, with no apparent signs of rancour. Didn't she mind that he hadn't come to her sooner? If she didn't then his cause was lost before he'd begun. Well, he wasn't going to grovel. He'd come the first moment he'd been able to.

'The men who tried to kidnap Melanie were apprehended. There were proceedings taken against them . . . and Marcha. Then I flew out to Italy, to see my father-in-law.'

He had Gina's interest now, at least. She was leaning slightly forward in her chair, even though she didn't speak.

'Mantalini was behind the attempt. Marcha *did* spend that holiday of hers in Italy . . . at La Spezia. Debbie and Steph were right; they did see her there.'

'But why?' Gina could keep silent no longer. 'Why should Marcha co-operate with him? How could she plot against you when she expected to marry you? It must have been planned before . . . before . . .'

'Before you came to Mallions and ousted her in my affections? Yes.'

'Then . . .'

'Marcha didn't intend her part in the kidnap to be known. That was part of her bargain with Mantalini. She didn't like children, didn't want to be bothered with mine. For some reason she believed she'd succeeded where others had failed, that she'd get me to marry her. With Melanie safely out of the way, she wouldn't have had to share my attention.'

'She admitted all that?'

'Not at first, no. Not until after I'd seen the Mantalini boys, heard their version. The sons weren't involved. They'd lost interest in their father's vendetta, so he'd relied on Marcha being on the inside ... and some hired bully boys.'

'How did he know about Marcha, contact her?'

'She knew about him, sought him out. She knew about his earlier attempts. Mantalini promised her money, too ... a great deal of it.'

'A circus performer with money?'

'Not only a performer ... a circus owner. He owned several. I say owned, because Mantalini is dead. Apparently when he heard about the failure of his latest coup, he flew into a rage which brought on a heart attack.'

'Good riddance!' Gina said feelingly and, at Tod's look of amazement, 'I can't feel sorry for him, or for Marcha. They've both caused too much trouble, too much heartache to people I . . .'

'Yes?' Tod said tensely as she broke off, her face flushing. Then, as she continued to stare up at him speechlessly, 'I suppose you weren't, by any chance, going to say "to people you love".'

She must brazen it out. There was a piece of sophistry she could employ.

'I adore Rusty, you know that ... and I became very fond of Melanie,' she added primly. Somehow she managed to look away from those penetrating dark eyes.

'Is that all?' His voice was harsh.

'What else should there be?' A nice, understated little note of surprise, she congratulated herself.

'Where do I come into all this?' he demanded and her stomach seemed to achieve several rapid backflips. Automatically, she rested her hand upon it, thinking of the growing life within, found Tod watching the gesture and as hastily withdrew it.

'I'm sorry, of course, that you had all that worry. But it's over now, isn't it?'

'Not by a long way!' He ground the words out savagely and bent forward leaning over her, his hands grasping her shoulders. 'I've had some worry in my life . . . but nothing worries me so damned much as you do.'

She refused to look at him, felt she couldn't speak. But that insidious trembling had begun to agitate her body and he must be aware of it. She must say something, if only to divert his attention, to give herself breathing space.

'What I can't understand,' she said, amazed at the controlled note of her own voice, as if she were merely discussing some academic problem, 'is why you wanted me as Marcha's stand-in, when she was so against it.'

The diversion worked, temporarily. His grasp relaxed a little.

'Whatever her opinion,' he said simply, 'she needed you. There was no one else who resembled her so closely to be found at such short notice, and there was no way I could get her to perform her own stunts. When she realised I didn't intend to back down, she added to what she'd already told me of your background a very elaborate tissue of lies and insinuations, so that I'd be very disinclined to believe anything you might have let slip about *her*. If it hadn't been for young Rusty . . . I'm glad I decided to visit him again.'

'Why did you?'

'For his own sake, initially . . . I liked the lad, admired his guts . . . and to find out more about you. In so doing, I uncovered Marcha's lies, her true nature. And now, Gina, let's stop shilly-shallying. When are you coming back to Mallions ... to Rusty ... to *me*?' The blunt, uncompromising question took her by surprise.

'Never! There's no reason why I should. I completed my part of your film and I told you I wouldn't work for you again, even if you did try to sue me for breach of contract.'

'Gina! Being a businesswoman seems to be bad for you. Will you please stop looking at everything in terms of pounds and pence? I don't care a damn if you never appear in another film, and one thing's certain, there'll be no more stunting for you.'

'Why?' she asked suspiciously, disregarding the first part of his sentence. Had he any idea? No, he couldn't have.

'Because I've watched one woman I love kill herself. I don't intend to let that happen again.'

It was not stubbornness, nor was it pique that kept her silent now. He had, effectively, taken away her breath.

'Did you hear what I said?' he demanded, giving her a little shake.

'I heard!' she managed to say.

'Well?'

'Well what? Do you expect me to fall at your feet in gratitude? I've told you, on several occasions, I don't like your ideas about love. OK. So you're rid of Marcha ... well rid. You must know plenty of other women who are panting to take her place. But I'm not one of them.'

'Is it this damned stupid idea you have that you're first and foremost a career woman? Because, if so, I'll tell you now, I won't interfere with that. You can keep your agency, be financially independent if you like. You can act ... you can do anything you damned well please, just so long as you come back to me.'

He was making it very difficult for her. He was offering her everything she had ever wanted, except for one thing. He wanted her on his terms, without commitment, without marriage. She was glad he didn't know about the baby. He might have felt compelled to offer marriage then, just to gain control of his future son or daughter. But she wouldn't have wanted those sort of terms either.

'Gina!' His voice grated huskily in his throat. 'Come back. I want you with me. I need you.' He pulled her up out of the chair, so that they stood breast to breast, thigh to thigh. 'I'll *make* you come back,' he told her savagely. 'I'll make you want me again. If I have to I'll even resort to Mantalini's tricks, I'll abduct you. If I once get you back to Mallions, you'll never escape me again. I'll keep you where you belong, in my bed, until you give in.' He scooped her up, ignoring her protesting cries, but instead of heading for the door, as she had feared, he carried her in the direction of her bedroom.

As he dumped her on the bed he looked around him.

'Very pretty! But it's a woman's idea of what a bedroom should be. It's obvious no man has ever been in here. Well I can think of a far better setting in which to make love to you, but for now, this will do!'

It was of no avail to struggle, to protest. She couldn't overcome his determination that way. She'd failed before. She had to use a surer deterrent, one which would appeal to his reason.

'OK,' she said wearily. 'I know in this kind of situation I lose out. I know you can make me want you ... you've proved that often enough. But however many times you do that, you'll always end up the loser, because however much I might enjoy your lovemaking, however much I might crave for it, you'll never get me back to Mallions willingly.' She flung out her arms dramatically. 'Well ... go on then ... get on with it ... and then go.'

'Damn you, Gina!' He sat down on the edge of the

bed. 'You certainly know how to turn a man off. For God's sake, I don't want to take you against your will. I want your co-operation, not . . . not a sacrificial victim. Just tell me what you've got against me, why you can't love me as well as want me? Is it my past, the women since . . . since Maria? I can tell you, they didn't mean a damned thing. They were just to . . . to save me from going out of my mind.'

'And that's all I'd be.' She sat up. 'Don't you see, Tod? I don't want that casual kind of relationship. I don't want to be something you just use when your body is in need. My ideal is to be a companion to a man, friend as well as lover, to have shared interests, respect . . .'

'Hold on! Hold on!' There was a queer kind of urgency in his voice. 'What you're trying to tell me is that *you* want marriage?'

'Yes. And since you don't . . .'

'Shut up! What the hell do you think I've been trying to say all this time . . . the last time we made love? I told you then that I loved you. I think I must have been in love with you for a long time, only I'd forgotten what the sensation felt like.'

'You said,' Gina told him disbelievingly, accusingly, 'that you'd no intention of marrying . . . Marcha or anyone else.'

'That's true, but you didn't let me finish. I meant anyone else but you. But you got hysterical. You let me see just why you had this block against men, because you could never get pregnant. Gina, I know I told you I wanted a son, but it doesn't matter. It's not important, not as important as having you. I've got one child. We'll share her. I'll . . . I'll adopt Rusty. I'd thought of it anyway. Gina, please say you'll marry me. Put me out of this torture I've been going through for the last few weeks, not able to come to you, wondering if you were all right. I didn't even know for a while whether you'd landed that blasted plane safely, if I'd ever see you again. And now I'm here, now I've found you, I'm no better off. It ... it's like beating my head against a brick wall.'

'Tod!' She'd said his name twice already, trying to stem the flow of his words. Now, finally, 'Shut up!' Surprised into silence, he did. 'Shut up, Tod, and let me get a word in. If you hadn't gone raving on, you could have had at least five minutes less uncertainty. I haven't got a block against men, certainly not against one particular man ... you. I love you, Tod, and if you'd said "marry me" as soon as you walked through that front door, instead of ... well ... Anyway, I'd have said "yes" right away.'

He swallowed.

'You would?' Then, with more certainty, 'You would, Gina?'

'It was all I wanted to hear, idiot!' she told him affectionately.

'I *am* an idiot, aren't I?' he admitted. 'But it never occurred to me that your response to me was anything other than a physical one.'

'It seems to me,' she said softly, 'that there's only one way I can prove it to you.' She held out her arms and he came down into them willingly. Her mouth sought his, warmly, eagerly. 'I love you, Tod Fallon. I loved you long before I even *liked* you.'

He could not doubt her sincerity as he felt the shudders that began to run through her, as she sought to pull him closer. Exultantly he gathered her up, demonstrating the full force of his arousal as they kissed until both were breathless.

Without relinquishing her mouth, he began to undo the buttons of the severe grey dress, dispensed with her bra, his fingers caressing with tactile intimacy.

'Gina?' It was a question that needed no enlargement.

'Yes!' she whispered. 'Oh, yes, Tod. Oh Tod, I *ache* so. Please . . . please . . .'

Gently he removed her clothes, swiftly discarded his own, lowered his weight upon her once more.

'I never intended to fall in love again,' he said ruefully between kisses, 'but I think I knew right from the first that I was lost, only I wouldn't admit it to myself. I thought it was just physical . . . for both of us. But I know now this *is* love. Gina, please tell me you believe me.'

'I believe you,' she told him.

Then he made love to her, a desperate, starved, devouring love, their gasps turning to groans of delight at the pleasures that racked their bodies, pleasure neither had thought to know again . . . together. Then he entered her warmth, raised her, possessed her, his movements increasing their rapidity as she urged herself against him, ending in a shuddering, convulsive climax that transcended even their first coming together, since now they both knew the ecstasy was born, not only of wanting, but of love.

They lay still for a while, glorying in the continuing contact.

'Happy?' Tod asked after a while.

'Completely. You're my whole life, from this moment on.'

He laughed softly, a gentle, contented sound, but it held disbelief.

'Knowing you, I'll have to move over to leave room for that career of yours.'

'Maybe! But not for a while. I think my time will be pretty full, between you . . . and your son.'

'My son?' He raised himself to look at her. 'Gina, if you only knew how I wish . . . A child of our love. But you told me it was impossible.'

'I know. I thought it was. But it seems it isn't. Oh, Tod . . .' Her eyelids fluttered down shyly. 'I'm . . . I'm six weeks pregnant.'

An urgent hand grasped her chin.

'Is this true?' he rasped. 'Why didn't you tell me before? God, if I've harmed you . . .'

'Harmed me?' Her green eyes were brilliant with happy tears. 'Tod, your love can only do me good, better than any medication. In fact . . .' Her mouth curved into a wicked little smile as her hands issued an unmistakable invitation.

'Witch! Temptress!' he gasped. 'Oh, Gina, my love. You can't want it any more than I do. But are you sure?'

'Quite sure,' she said serenely.

He was gentle this time, reverent almost, but nonetheless satisfying to her senses, to his own.

'You were misnamed,' he whispered, as once more they lay in peaceful aftermath. 'Not fantasy, but fantastic . . . *my* Fantastic Woman!'

ROMANCE

Merry Christmas
one and all.

CHANCES ARE
Barbara Delinsky

ONE ON ONE
Jenna Lee Joyce

AN IMPRACTICAL PASSION
Vicki Lewis Thompson

A WEEK FROM FRIDAY
Georgia Bockoven

THE GIFT OF HAPPINESS
Amanda Carpenter

HAWK'S PREY
Carole Mortimer

TWO WEEKS TO REMEMBER
Betty Neels

YESTERDAY'S MIRROR
Sophie Weston

More choice for the Christmas stocking. Two special reading packs from Mills & Boon. Adding more than a touch of romance to the festive season.

AVAILABLE: OCTOBER, 1986   PACK PRICE: £4.80

ACCEPT 4
MILLS & BOON
ROMANCES
ABSOLUTELY FREE

...after all, what better way to continue your enjoyment of the finest stories from the world's foremost romantic authors? This is a very special introductory offer designed for regular readers. Once you've read your four **free** books you can take out a subscription (although there's no obligation at all). Subscribers enjoy many special benefits and all these are described overleaf. ►►►

Mills & Boon